# SILENCING SALTER

---

A LUCA MYSTERY
BOOK 7

DAN PETROSINI

Print ISBN: 978-1-960286-09-3
Naples, FL
Library of Congress Control Number: 2023901525

# ACKNOWLEDGMENTS

Special thanks to Julie, Stephanie and Jennifer for their love and support, and thanks to Squad Sergeant Craig Perrilli for his counsel on the real world of law enforcement. He helps me keep it real.

# OTHER BOOKS BY DAN

**THE LUCA MYSTERY SERIES**

Am I the Killer

Vanished

The Serenity Murder

Third Chances

A Cold, Hard Case

Cop or Killer?

Silencing Salter

A Killer Missteps

Uncertain Stakes

The Grandpa Killer

Dangerous Revenge

Where Are They

Buried at the Lake

The Preserve Killer

No One is Safe

**SUSPENSEFUL SECRETS**

Cory's Dilemma

Cory's Flight

Cory's Shift

**OTHER WORKS BY DAN PETROSINI**

The Final Enemy

Complicit Witness

Push Back

Ambition Cliff

# 1

I WAS FEELING UNNERVED AND COULDN'T PUT MY FINGER ON why. Our baby girl, Jessica, was a bundle of joy, and Mary Ann and I were enjoying our new roles as parents. The concerns I had about fatherhood cramping my relationship with my wife were unfounded. So far. Even the intermittent pain in my gut had gone away.

Life was good. I couldn't imagine things being sweeter than they were. So why did it feel like I was standing on a wakeboard? Something seemed to lurk just below the surface. I wasn't a stranger to the feeling, but it was usually a result of a pending problem, like the dissolving situation with my ex-wife, my ex-partner ending up dead, and dealing with my cancer.

We'd run out of diapers, and I had to make a run to Walmart before going to the office. A new website for infant supplies had great prices but terrible delivery service. Handing off an armful of diapers to Mary Ann, I hopped back in the Cherokee and headed to work.

Derrick called as I drove past Bayfront.

"What's up?"

"You on the way in?"

"Yep, about to turn onto Forty-One. Why?"

"Call came in about a body."

I knew it. "Where?"

"In the back of a place called Stone Heaven. It's a granite warehouse on J and C Boulevard."

"Text me the address, and I'll head straight there. Make sure someone cordons off the property. I don't want anyone within a hundred feet of the corpse."

Turning onto Airport Pulling Road, I realized it was February 20th, and spring was a month away. Instead of things turning greener, they had taken a turn toward darkness.

———

THREE SQUAD CARS were parked in front of Stone Heaven. I didn't see Derrick's car. The property wasn't gated. The weight of the slabs on display would nix any threat of their being stolen.

A uniformed officer lifted up the crime scene tape. Scooting under, the pain in my abdomen resurfaced. Signing in, I was grateful I had an appointment with the doctor who'd removed my bladder.

Walking up the drive, I couldn't detect any camera surveillance. There was an array of slabs the size of garage doors in different shades of white, some with dark gray veins and others pure.

The building was a two-storied industrial affair with the front softened to accommodate a small showroom. Peering through the glass revealed two desks fronted with chairs and displays that reminded me of a tile store. Other than that, it was bare bones.

Along the right side of the building was a narrow parking

lot. Toward the back were scores of thin slabs standing inches from each other. It looked like a giant deck of cards spread out. A pair of officers stood guard about ten yards in. I had played softball with one of them when I first got down to Naples. He was a good guy but a world-class wiseass.

"Hey, Frank. How are you? Heard you're all domesticated now, with a wife and baby."

"That's right. And how you been keeping, Dillon?"

"All is good. We can use a second baseman this year, if you're not changing diapers."

"Ha-ha. What do we have?"

"Delivery crew was loading the day's slabs, and the guy working the forklift, Julio Barza, found the body."

"Anybody touch anything?"

"No. The guy said he jumped off the forklift and ran into the warehouse to get the foreman." He pointed. "The body is just past the black slab."

There was a larger space in between the slabs, and the body was lying facedown on top of a couple of empty slab cradles. I noticed it right away.

It looked like a professional hit: hands bound, bullet in the back of the head, duct tape over the mouth. The victim was a white male, late forties to early fifties. Six foot, a hundred and eighty or so pounds. I crouched. He had good skin and was well groomed.

I put the back of my fist on the victim's right hand. It was cool. I moved my fist to his midsection. There wasn't much give. He was dead at least several hours. Maybe killed somewhere between 1 and 5 a.m.

The victim was wearing a long-sleeved white shirt, dark blue slacks, and expensive loafers. I put on gloves and checked his rear pockets. Nothing. Did people with his kind of money not need to carry a wallet, or was this a robbery?

Taking the time to put a body in a place like this didn't fit a random robbery. Whoever killed this guy likely took his identity to buy time and grab a little cash.

The forensics team would have a mobile fingerprint scanner. Maybe we'd get a quick hit on an ID. I circled the body. The blood pattern indicated he'd been dumped here. Just in case, I scanned for a shell, knowing if he were shot here, whoever did this wouldn't leave one behind.

Who was this man? Why was he shot in the back of the head, like a mob slaying? I knew stereotypes were out, but the victim didn't look like the organized-crime type.

Maybe it was my time in New Jersey, but no matter how slick someone dressed and was groomed, I could tell if they were gangsters, seeing right through their Brooks Brothers costumes.

They were the personification of the old adage: you can put lipstick on a pig, but it is still a pig. No matter how many manicures they sat for or silk suits they wore, nothing could soften their hearts.

I'd have to turn my badge in if the man lying here was a gangster. It didn't fit. Who was this guy, and why was he executed? I walked to the rear of the property, which didn't have a fence. It backed up to a building with four small businesses: a computer repair shop, a decorator, a music store, and an accounting office.

The property to the left was a body shop, and to the right was a plumbing supply house. This was a busy industrial area, and I hoped we would get an eyewitness or two. I walked out front and waited for the forensics crew.

**2**

———————

"HAPPY BIRTHDAY, LITTLE PEANUT. I CAN'T BELIEVE YOU'RE four months old already."

I took Jessica from Mary Ann, kissing her on both cheeks. She was beautiful. A real-life angel with blond hair and chubby cheeks. She looked like a lighter-colored version of my wife. Jessie started to cry. I handed her back to Mary Ann, and she settled down immediately.

I extended a finger hoping Jessie would grab it. "What do you have, some magic or something?"

"She's just tired. I was about to put her in for a nap, but I heard the garage door."

I leaned in and inhaled. Babies had a smell of their own and it was intoxicating. "You have a good nap, Daddy. I'll see you later, okay?"

"You've got to cut out the daddy stuff. She'll get confused over her name."

"That's ridiculous."

"Let me get her settled in while you change."

Heading into the bedroom, I noticed the time. It was only 5:30 p.m. I didn't know if it was Jessie or the need for an ID on the body before we could hunt down the killer, but I was guilt free leaving work at five.

The corpse was the first homicide since Jessica was born. There were many unknowns in the new case, and chief among them was whether I could maintain a proper family/work balance.

Mary Ann tiptoed into the room, her shoulders scrunched toward her ears. Why did people do that? Did they really think they were lighter on their feet by holding their shoulders up?

"She fell asleep as soon as I put her down."

"Is she coming down with something?"

"No. She didn't sleep that long this afternoon. You should have seen her. She was babbling every time I put the mobile on."

"I bet she's gonna talk early. Last night she was trying to say daddy when you were showering."

"Keep dreaming, Frank."

"No, I swear. It sounded like she was trying to say dada."

"Maybe because you keep calling her daddy."

"Very funny. Should I put the grill on?"

"I took some shrimp out of the freezer. I'll heat up the soup from yesterday."

It was the third time in a week we were having shrimp. I wanted to run to Burger King and pick up a Whopper and fries, but Mary Ann was trying to get back into shape, and I had to support her. I went out to the lanai knowing I'd get my burger for lunch tomorrow.

When I came back in, Mary Ann had the TV on but it was muted. I pointed to a picture to the left of the newscaster.

"Who's that man?"

"I don't know. Why?"

"He looks like the guy we found dead on J and C Boulevard this morning."

"Homicide?"

"No doubt. Looked like a professional hit." I grabbed the remote, raising the volume.

"Frank!"

The picture of the man disappeared, replaced by a weather map. I began cycling through channels, hoping to see what may have been our victim's face. Mary Ann took the remote and shut the TV.

"You want to eat with Jessie in your lap? Because I'm not gonna hold her."

"Okay, okay."

------

JESSIE HAD GOTTEN up only twice during the night. My deal with Mary Ann was she would get up first, and then we'd rotate. It was crazy, but I never minded getting up for her. It was like we had our own special time together in the middle of the night. The kid was amazing.

The coffee Derrick had brought me was lukewarm. I got up to take it to the cafeteria when my desk phone rang.

"Detective Luca, homicide."

"Frank, it's Dr. Esposito."

It was the pathologist. "How you doing, Doc?"

"I'm about to begin the postmortem examination. I'm pretty sure I know who the victim is."

"You do?"

"I'm pretty sure it's Elby Salter."

"How do you spell that?"

I jotted down the name, asking, "What makes you think it's him?"

"My brother-in-law sponsored a table at the Ritz for the Cure Cancer Gala a couple of months ago. Maggie and I went, and Elby Salter was either the chair or co-chair of the event."

I plugged Elby Salter into the search bar and went to the image results. A series of photos of a man in tuxedos appeared. He didn't resemble the man I saw on TV last night.

"How sure are you?"

"Just about positive. I saw him one other time, years ago. The Salters are an old Florida family, very wealthy, and Elby was always doing one charity thing or another. I hope it's not him, but . . ."

"All right, then. We'll reach out to the family. See if he's reported missing. I'll let you know if we come up with anything. Meanwhile, conduct the autopsy, and let me know what you find. It'd be nice if you'd come up with something to help make it a quick solve."

Handing the name to Derrick, I said, "Get ahold of the family. Find out if Elby Salter is missing. Esposito thinks it could be the corpse. I'm going to heat up my coffee."

Walking down the hallway, I had the feeling it was him. If so, we knew who the victim was. Now we needed to find out why he was shot and who did it.

**3**

———————

Derrick met me in the hallway. "Looks like Elby Salter is missing. His wife said she hasn't seen him in two days."

"She file a missing person?"

He shook his head. "She said she knew you couldn't file one until someone was missing four days."

"What? That never stopped anyone."

"She said she assumed he was with his mistress."

"For two nights? That's one hell of a marriage."

"They're wealthy. Maybe she's hanging around for the money."

"Or she has a boyfriend of her own."

"They call that an open marriage."

"I call it crazy. Did you tell her we needed her to look at the body and see if it's him?"

"Yeah, said she would swing by the medical examiner's in an hour or so."

"Don't tell me she said, 'swing by'?"

"That's how she put it."

"Call Esposito; tell him she's coming in. I don't want him slicing and dicing this guy up before the wife gets there."

"I'm on it."

"What's the wife's name?"

"Annabelle."

"Annabelle. Pretty name. It was one of the names Mary Ann liked. Can't imagine Jessie as an Annabelle now."

"You made the right choice. I like Jessica better."

"I'm gonna head down to the morgue, talk it over with Esposito while I wait for her to show up. He should have a time of death for us."

I PULLED on the sweater I kept in the trunk and buttoned my blazer before entering the low-slung building housing Collier's medical examiner. It still felt cold. Dr. Esposito was in his office. Jamming my hands into my pockets, I headed down a windowless corridor to the pathologist's office.

A coffee mug, pronouncing, *Medical Examiners Do It with a Scalpel,* sat on the corner of the doctor's desk. Esposito was wearing headphones, tapping away on a keyboard. He raised his head, sticking a finger up. He typed a couple of words more before removing the headphones.

"How are you, Frank?"

"All is good."

"How's the new baby?"

I smiled. "Pretty amazing, if I say so myself."

"It's a gift from God."

I pulled my phone out. "Here she is."

"You have a cute one there, Frank. I see a lot of you in her, some of your resemblance to George Clooney. Enjoy it while it lasts."

While it lasts? "We are."

"Derrick said Elby Salter hadn't been seen, and his wife is coming down. Looks like you were right."

"It's a damn shame. He's only fifty-three."

"Doc, you have a time of death for me?"

"Somewhere between one and two a.m., the morning of February twentieth."

"Okay. It's obvious, but I have to ask: cause of death?"

"Gunshot wound in the rear of the head. I'd guess it was a .357 or maybe a .44, but I'm not going to remove it until the next of kin confirms the identity."

"I know you didn't start, but is there anything you can tell me?"

"An examination exteriorly didn't indicate anything extraordinary. An abdominal scar that appears to have originated from a hernia procedure and one on the knee that was probably the result of a surgical repair of his ACL."

"No bruises. To the head or body?"

"None."

The victim had been surprised by his attackers or knew them. He didn't resist or need to be silenced. Someone could have approached from behind, stuck the barrel of the gun in his back, and walked him into a car or van, where he was bound.

"I'd appreciate if you'd do a full blood workup. If it's Elby Salter, he had money, and there's no telling what substance he might have been taking."

"It's not likely he was taking an illegal substance."

"What makes you say that?"

"First, he appears to be in excellent health, and second, they're not the type to run around in public. They're a private, low-key family."

I didn't want to insult the doctor by challenging his ignorance. "Let's see what the blood panels tell us, if anything."

Esposito's phone rang. Mrs. Annabelle Salter was here. I hadn't spoken to her and knew nothing about this woman, but that hadn't stopped me from forming a mental image of her.

THERE WERE two women in the lobby. The first thought to pop in my head was *The Stepford Wives*. I'd never seen the movie or even knew what it was about. I approached the women hoping I'd remember to check into the movie. The women had similar faces and builds. They appeared related and were dressed in an understated style, both in dark pants, one with a short jacket over a white blouse, the other wearing a long-sleeved, cream-colored blouse. They had the same honey-colored hair and were wearing low, leather pumps.

"Hello, ladies. I'm Detective Frank Luca."

The woman wearing the jacket stepped forward, extending her hand. "Annabelle Salter. It is a pleasure to meet you. This is my sister, Savannah."

I noticed a tremble in her hand before shaking it. "I wish it were under different circumstances, ma'am."

Annabelle gave a short nod. "Shall we?"

They had no idea where they were going, but I heard myself say, "After you." I stepped aside, then said, "It's the third door on the right."

Savannah grabbed her sister's hand as they stopped in front of a door marked *Private*. Circling in front of them, I asked, "Ready?"

Annabelle bit her lower lip and nodded. I swung the door open to a small room. A translucent window dominated the left wall. A pair of couches lined the opposite wall.

Closing the door behind them, I stepped to the side of the window. I put my hand on a wall switch. "Ready?"

Annabelle took a deep breath. "Okay."

I threw the switch, and the window cleared. A sheet covered the body on the gurney. Dr. Esposito stood by the corpse's shoulders, looking me in the eye. I nodded, and he pulled the sheet back, revealing the head.

A gasp, then, "Oh my God, Elby." Annabelle began crying, and her sister led her away from the window as Esposito covered Elby Salter's face.

"Would you like to sit?"

She shook her head.

"Is that your husband, Elby Salter?"

Lips quivering. "Yes."

"Why don't you take your sister home, and we'll talk later if she's up to it?"

---

Derrick said, "How'd it go?"

"Let's just say it's the shittiest part of the job, but we know it's Elby Salter for sure."

"Look, a call came in. Some guy walking his dog on J & C that night thinks he saw something."

"Now we're talking. What'd he say?"

"His dog was taking a dump right by Stone Heaven, and he saw a white Explorer pull into the driveway."

"Did he see anyone?"

"Yeah. I'm bringing him in to work with a sketch artist."

"Maybe we'll get lucky."

**4**

————

I HUNG UP MY JACKET, AND LOOSENING MY TIE, SAID, "Derrick, we need to know as much as possible about Elby Salter. I want to know everything he did the last forty-eight hours before he was killed. Who he was with, where he was. Check his credit cards, phone records, the whole works."

"I'm on it. After you called, I did an internet search. The Salter family has Florida roots going back to when Florida became a state. I don't know if it's bullshit or not, but did you know Florida had its own currency before it became a state?"

"No idea. What else did you learn?"

"There's not much out there. He's the son of Delilah and Prescott Salter. I found an obit for the mother but nothing on the old man. They had another son, Chadwick, and he and Elby control a company called Southern Motor Works. They own a bunch of car dealerships all over the state. There was mention of a couple of real estate developments he was a part of, something about him trying to get the Red Sox to move to Naples, and a bunch of charity stuff."

"Where do they work out of?"

"I don't know. I don't remember anything about a head-quarters or anything."

I went to the whiteboard, picked up an orange marker, and wrote *Elby,* and circled it. I drew a line to the left and wrote *Annabelle/wife.* To the right, *Chadwick/brother.* Underneath it, *business.*

"Get pictures of the three of them up here. That's where we're gonna start. First up is the wife. You get going with credit cards and phone records. I'm going to get some background on Annabelle before going to see her. By the way, you said she seemed cavalier about his disappearance when you called her, right?"

"Yeah. I was kind of shocked."

"She played it pretty near perfect today."

"What do you mean? You think she was faking it?"

"I don't know what I mean, just that she was reserved, appropriate."

"Being in a morgue can do that to you."

"Yep. Get to work."

I pulled up the marriage license for Annabelle and Elby Salter. They were married twenty-three years ago, when Elby was thirty and his new bride, twenty-five. Annabelle's maiden name was Baker. I noted the information on the application, including her home at the time.

The address listed was deeded to Thomas and Mavis Baker. They had to be her parents. I went to Google Earth. What came up was an immense property with several build-ings. Money had married money.

THE SALTER'S home was on high-end Gordon Drive. I called it millionaire's row. Rumor had it that more Fortune 500

CEOs lived in the Naples area than in any other place in the country. Given New York, Greenwich, San Francisco, and other wealthy enclaves, I wasn't sure, but if true, it was likely they'd be living on Gordon Drive.

Passing one behemoth home after another, I slowed as the addresses got closer to my destination. Expecting a gaudy entrance, I double-checked the address of the ungated driveway that was my target.

Fifty yards up the gravel driveway, it ended in a T. I looked straight ahead, squinting as the Gulf of Mexico reflected the sun. The driveway to the left led to a large Georgian Colonial. I noticed a weathered, circular plaque with an arrow pointing left. It read *Elby and Annabelle*. I searched for a sign as to what the right driveway led to but couldn't find anything. There was a house in that direction, but it was obscured by a stand of fantail palm trees.

I headed toward the yellow mansion, wondering how nice it would be to sit on one of those porches, wine glass in hand, and stare at the Gulf. The two-storied home had porches on both levels encircling the building, with round columns supporting the expansive overhang. My first thought was the movie *Gone with the Wind*. I couldn't tell you why, because I hadn't seen that movie either.

Though the landscaping was minimal, there was a lot to take in. Fronting the home was a fountain in the shape of a dolphin surrounded by a bed of purple flowers. Two dormers on the slope of the home's roof looked like a pair of frog's eyes. A tennis court was off to the right and a pool area to the left.

Even though the home and setting were extraordinary, there was a normalcy about the property. You couldn't say it wasn't maintained, it was, but not to the polished level of the beachfront homes along Gordon Drive.

As I realized the home was understated, like the woman I met today, the front door swung out. The dead man's sister-in-law, Savannah, waved.

"How is your sister feeling?"

"She's doing well. I guess . . ."

"I know it may seem inconsiderate, but it's best that I speak with her as soon as possible."

"Annabelle is aware the police need to speak to her. She's 'round back, on the veranda."

Veranda? It was a porch. A damn nice porch, but a porch. I was disappointed that she walked me around the porch rather than through the house. You never know what you can learn by seeing the inside of a victim's home. But, the truth was, the real reason I was upset was not getting a chance to see what the place looked like.

We passed several comfortable groups of seating on our way to the back. Spinning overhead fans were hung every twenty feet. The house was almost as deep as it was wide. The view of the Gulf expanded with every step. A few steps from the rear, I saw Annabelle. She was wearing a flowery dress that fit the surroundings but was off, given the circumstances.

She rose to greet me. Her eyes were red.

"Welcome to our home, Detective."

"I appreciate your willingness to talk so soon after the . . ."

"May I offer you a glass of lemonade?"

"That sounds nice."

Savannah disappeared into the house, and Annabelle said, "Please. Take a seat."

Her teeth were white but not veneers. She was wearing pearl earrings but no other jewelry except a simple wedding band. I couldn't recall if she had it on earlier today. There was something about this woman. I could feel her pull.

"I know this is difficult for you, but finding the person who did this is easier the sooner we start."

"Strike while the iron's hot, I guess."

Savannah appeared out of nowhere with a glass of lemonade on a tray.

"Thank you." I took the ice-cold glass. Taking a sip, I saw Savannah slip back into the house. She wanted no part of this. Or was it respect for her sister's privacy?

I put the glass down. "Tell me about your husband, Elby."

"Well, there's not much to say. We met at my cousin Magnolia's wedding and were married a year later."

"Any children?"

"No. I'm afraid not."

I wanted to tell her she didn't know what she was missing, but it was early in the game for me. "What did your husband do for a living?"

"The Salter family has various business interests."

"I know he is involved in automotive dealerships. What else?"

"Real estate, farming, manufacturing, just about anything you could imagine."

Did that signal something illegitimate? I reached for my glass. It was wet with condensation. If you looked up the word refreshing, there might be a picture of my lemonade.

"Was he actively running any particular business?"

"I wouldn't characterize it as running a business, more akin to strategic oversight. Elby was focused on long-range planning. He'd never miss his monthly strategy meetings, no matter what was going on."

"What interests or hobbies did your husband engage in?"

"Besides chairing several charities, Elby had an addiction to baseball, in particular the Boston Red Sox."

"Was he from Boston?"

"Heavens, no. He was born and raised right here. On this very property."

"Oh. So, why the Boston Red Sox?"

"I'm not sure. It could be the family had a home on Martha's Vineyard, but it probably had to do with the origins of the American Revolution."

I wanted to ask whether he was one of those guys who dressed up and reenacted scenes from the fight for independence but didn't.

"Tell me about any possible enemies Elby might have had."

"Enemies? We're speaking of Elby. Everybody loved Elby."

"No problems with business partners?"

"Elby never discussed business with me. It was a Salter family rule. Business was a family subject. If you weren't born a Salter, you weren't family, even when you married into the family."

It sounded strange, but I could see the wealthy being sensitive about outsiders.

"When my partner called you this morning, I believe you made a reference about your husband possibly being with another woman."

"The Salter men have a history of playing the field, regardless of their marital status."

"Was there one particular woman he spent time with recently?"

"You'd have to ask his brother about that."

"Chadwick?"

"Yes."

If she were bothered enough to kill her husband over his philandering, it didn't show. It must have been going on for years. That left money as possible motivation for Annabelle to have her husband killed. It didn't seem likely, as her parents seemed to be well off, but I couldn't rule it out.

Time and time again, two constants in a homicide were that the killer was usually close to the victim and that the motivation was greed. I wanted to ask her about a prenuptial but couldn't imagine a family like the Salters not insisting on one. It was a question the brother would be able to answer.

"Do you know your husband's whereabouts the day he was murdered?"

Her lip quivered. "It felt like a normal day. We had breakfast out here and he left."

"For work?"

"I assumed so."

"How was he dressed?"

"Dress shirt and slacks but no tie."

"Did he usually wear a tie?"

"No, he detested wearing a tie."

"When did you expect him home?"

"He said he had a dinner meeting in Fort Myers."

"Was that unusual?"

"No. But frankly, it could have been cover for a rendezvous with a lady friend."

"We may need your assistance in obtaining access to his phone records. They could provide critical information. Would you be willing to help if we need it?"

"Yes. Of course."

I asked a few more incidental questions, finished my lemonade and took another look at the Gulf before leaving. After learning more about Elby Salter, I'd be back with more questions for Annabelle.

**5**

---

Jessica was sound asleep in her bassinet. Mary Ann took one more look at her and climbed into bed. On my way out of the bathroom, I adjusted the thermostat.

"Did you lower the air?"

"Yep."

"I don't want it too cold for her."

"I set it at seventy-four."

"Good. She should be okay."

I hopped in bed, fishing the remote off the nightstand. "It's hot. I put the fan on low."

"Okay." Mary Ann rolled on her side and kissed my cheek. "Love you. Good night."

"You know we should get a will made up."

"A will?"

"Yeah, we have Jessie now . . ."

"Are you worried because you had cancer?"

Even though I was, I said, "It's not just that. Something could happen to both of us, then what? Who would take care of Jessica? Who'd she live with?"

Mary Ann propped herself on an elbow. "Is everything all right with you, Frank?"

I hoped so but was filled with doubt. "Calm down. I'm talking about Jessica. We have a responsibility to provide for her. Frankly, we've been irresponsible. Shit happens out of nowhere, and I don't want just anybody as her guardian."

"You're right. This needs a lot of thought. God forbid it comes down to that. I don't know who I'd want her to live with. I can't even think like that."

"We have to."

"Who were you thinking of?"

"I don't know. The only two people I can think of right now are Derrick and the Blazers."

"Derrick's not even married. Jeanie and Paul have Brian, and they are wonderful parents."

"We don't really know them, Mary Ann. I know Derrick; he's my partner."

She smiled. "You really have let the whole Garrison thing go, haven't you?"

"The kid made a mistake. He's a good person, ethically and morally. I think if anything happened to us, he'd step up and take care of Jessie. I really do."

"He's not married yet, and he has no experience bringing a child up."

"What? We didn't have any experience, no new parent does."

"I know that. It's not that, it's . . ."

"I get it. It's because he's a man."

She averted her eyes. "No. No, that's not true."

It was true. "It's okay, Mary Ann. I get it. A mother is special. You couldn't imagine a man doing what you do. You're right, but Lynn will make a good mother, and Jessie really seems to like her."

"I like her, but . . ."

"This is as important as it gets. Let's think about it and talk it over this week. Okay?"

"It's a scary thing to think about, but thanks for bringing it up."

I swung my legs off the bed.a "Sleep good."

"Where you going?"

I tiptoed over to the bassinet and stared at my little girl before climbing back in bed.

---

DERRICK SET a coffee on my desk. "Morning, Frank."

"Morning."

"Something the matter?"

I'd been staring at him, wondering what kind of parent he'd be. "No, no. Just thinking about Elby Salter."

"I have the phone records."

"Good." I raised the coffee to my mouth and paused. Maybe drinking too much coffee was what was bothering my stomach. I set the cup down.

"What's the matter? I put just a touch of milk in it, like you like it."

"My stomach has been bothering me."

"I saw you rubbing it yesterday."

"It's nothing, just nerves or something."

"You should get it checked out, Frank. You can't play around with these things, especially after what you went through."

Derrick really cared about me. It was another reason I thought he'd take care of Jessie if needed.

"I know. I made an appointment with the doctor."

"Good."

I needed a boost, and one more coffee couldn't hurt, could it? I took a sip of coffee and said, "Coffee is perfect, as usual. What do we have with the Salter numbers?"

"Two outgoing calls to Chadwick Salter, two to a Cindy Baylor, one to Prescott Salter, that's his father, right?

"Yes. What about inbound calls?"

"Incoming, there was a call from his wife, one from Chadwick, and four calls from Cindy Baylor. The day before there were also three calls from a Marie Redoux and a call from a Ronald Weaver. That's the same name as the guy who used to play first base for Boston."

"It could be him. His wife said Elby was a big baseball fan and loved the Red Sox."

"A lot of players, especially for Boston, live down here since they train in Fort Myers."

"Yep. The Sox and Minnesota are in Fort Myers, the Orioles in Sarasota, and the Yanks in Tampa."

"The Red Sox are building a new stadium in Collier. One of the things that came up when I searched the internet was something connecting Salter to the move."

"You said that. It made me remember seeing something on the tube about a deal for the land. It'll probably take two to three years to build it though."

"We should go to a game before spring training ends."

"Sounds like fun, maybe when they're playing the Yanks."

"That would be something, especially since Peters jumped ship going to the Yanks."

"What they give him, like twenty million a year?"

"Yep. Twenty-two million. It's getting nuts. I guess that's why the Red Sox let him go. I'll check later to see who's playing where."

"Okay. We have to start interviewing. I'd like to start with the brother, and I'm betting that Cindy Baylor was Elby's girlfriend."

"Probably. Do you think his wife was playing around too?"

"Normally, I'd say a woman like her wouldn't. But you never know. She may have done something out of revenge."

"And the only good revenge is one that's gone too far."

"Hey, that's my saying."

"And a good one. It's so true."

"You got to give me credit if you're gonna use my Luca-isms."

"Pure wisdom. I'm learning at the feet of a genuine master."

I tossed a ball of paper at him. "Let's get to work."

"What do you want me to do?"

"Come with me to see Cindy Baylor. Let's see if she's the girlfriend and what she has to say."

"I thought you wanted to start with the brother?"

"Changed it up. We may get something from her that will let us know if the brother is lying or covering something up."

The dull pain in my belly began to sharpen. "I'm gonna take a leak. Track her down while I'm gone."

**6**

---

STEPPING INTO A STALL, I WAS AHEAD OF SCHEDULE, BEATING my pee-pee alarm for the first time in a year. Why was I having issues? Was it the fact that I pushed way past the doctor's orders on taking a pee every couple of hours? Had I created whatever mess was brewing in my gut?

I was a father. I couldn't be taking chances with my health. It felt like this was a serious issue. Maybe the bladder they made for me was failing from abusing it. If it wasn't what I was starting to believe it was, and God was sounding a warning bell, I was going to listen.

Stroking my abdomen, I began thinking it was a mistake that we were waiting for Jessica to turn six months old before baptizing her. What if something happened? To me, or God forbid, our little angel. I didn't believe the church when they said unbaptized children who died went into limbo. It sounded made up and self-serving, but I didn't want to take chances.

I was going to talk with Mary Ann later and set a date as soon as the church could do it. We'd need someone to act as godparents. The question again was whom, I thought, as a trickle of urine came out.

As the flow increased, the pain in my belly dissipated. I was relieved it was going away but fearful that it confirmed something was wrong with my plumbing. I batted around calling the doctor to see if I could move up my appointment as I finished going.

After washing my hands, I sent Mary Ann a text telling her we had to talk about Jessica's christening later.

Derrick was glued to his screen. I hoped he wasn't getting addicted to the internet, like most of the country.

"You ready to roll?"

"The autopsy report came in from Esposito."

"Print a copy for the case file."

"Just kicked them out. They're sitting on the printer."

I grabbed a handful of warm papers off the printer and began reading as I walked back to my desk.

The bullet was a hollow-point .357 Magnum, the type that expanded upon entrance to cause maximum tissue damage. Elby Salter hadn't had a chance. The forensics team didn't find a shell at the scene. Whoever did it either collected the shell before leaving or used a revolver. I was sure it was a revolver. It looked professional, and anyone with experience would want to eliminate a chance of a link being made.

Gunshot residue was detected at the base of the skull. The gun was pressed against the skull when fired. The bullet's trajectory was forty degrees and was lodged in the precentral gyrus area of the frontal lobe. The cause of death was massive hemorrhaging.

No evidence of any foreign substances, legal or illegal, was found in the victim's system. Elby Salter wasn't doing drugs and wasn't drugged by his killer to subdue him. He knew the killer or was surprised and restrained by him. Elby

Salter had a trace amount of alcohol in his blood that Esposito estimated was caused by drinking less than a glass of an alcoholic beverage.

Other than the gunshot wound, there were no other abrasions, bruises, or lacerations on Elby Salter's body. His health was good overall, though he had a slightly enlarged liver and minor scarring on his lungs.

If he wasn't shot, Salter had a reasonable chance of living into his nineties. Instead of playing pickleball and reminiscing about the fortunate life he led, Salter was scheduled to be cremated tomorrow. There wasn't anything in the report that raised objections; I had to release the body to the family.

I stared at the photo of Elby Salter that Derrick had pasted to the whiteboard. How did this old-money guy get shot in the back of the head like a drug dealer? What happened, Elby? What mess did you get into?

"Derrick, you don't have to read through all the panels."

"I know that. I was just going over it again, didn't want to miss anything."

He was being careful. A good trait to have as a detective —and as a guardian. "The autopsy didn't give us anything more than we knew."

"He had a drink, or at least half of one."

"True. Knowing where he had it could help, but I'm thinking it was as simple as a glass of wine with lunch."

"Something could have happened at lunch, or he received a call during lunch that made him get up and leave. Maybe that's why he had only half a glass or so."

"That's possible, because his stomach was empty, but we'll find that out. If he were having lunch somewhere, that should be pretty easy to nail down. Let's go see Cindy Baylor."

Elby Salter's girlfriend lived in one of the single-family homes that had been built in the rear of Mercato. I remembered when the first of the white, Key West-styled houses went up. A sign stated prices starting at a million. The sign had been altered several times, and the last time I checked, the prices were sitting at $1.8 million. That was a crazy amount of dough to live next to a Whole Foods parking lot.

We pulled through the gate and Derrick said, "This is pretty cool back here."

It might have been his youth showing. "It's not for me. A hassle every time to get in out of here."

"It's not that bad. You can walk to all the places in Mercato. You don't even need your car to grocery shop."

I pulled up to Cindy Baylor's home. It was tucked at the end of the small community, and she had no one on one side. It was a nicer setup than I expected, but even if I hit the lottery, it wasn't for me.

Derrick hit the bell, and the marine-green door swung open.

Unsurprisingly, Cindy Baylor wasn't anything like Annabelle Salter. She was wearing cut-off jean shorts with a midthigh frayed hole and a silky, red blouse. It may have been her bloodshot eyes, but she looked vulnerable. Baylor wasn't trashy. She had an unmistakable magnetism to her. A sexual pull. Ten years ago, I may have made a run at her.

I introduced ourselves and was pleased that Derrick didn't reach out to shake her hand like I did. He used his head to think, unlike a lot of men.

"Come on in."

She showed us into an area with grass on the wall and low-slung chairs with chrome arms and legs. A blue bowl and a *Gulf Shore Life* magazine topped the Lucite table in the center of the seating area.

As I sat, I said, "We're sorry for your loss, but we have some questions for you."

"I understand. I can't believe it's real."

Derrick said, "How long were you seeing Elby Salter?"

"Just about four years."

"He buy this place for you?"

"Uh, he helped a little, my divorce settlement was almost enough to swing it."

I said, "How long ago was the divorce?"

"It finally went through last February."

Derrick said, "So, you were seeing Mr. Salter while you were married?"

Baylor narrowed her eyes but said nothing.

I said, "Mr. Salter placed two calls to you the day he was murdered. Can you tell us the nature of those calls?"

"You probably know that Elby and I talked almost every day. We were supposed to get together that night. He called me after the game and said he was going to a meeting and would call me later."

Derrick said, "Game?"

"A Red Sox spring training game. He and Ronnie went to almost every game."

Derrick asked, "Ronnie who?"

"Ron Weaver. He played for the Red Sox and is, like, the general manager now. He and Elby are good friends."

"Okay, go ahead."

"Well, he called again. I think it was about six p.m. He said he was hung up and would call me later. But he never did."

"And you called him four times?"

"What was I supposed to do? I was worried. Elby wasn't

perfect, but if he said he was going to do something, he did it."

I said, "There's nothing wrong with calling him."

A text message came in from Mary Ann. Jessica was running a fever, and she was at the pediatrician's office. I sent a text back asking how high the fever was running.

Derrick said, "What do you know about any enemies Elby Salter had?"

"I, I don't know anything about that. He was a kind man. I mean, he was headstrong a lot of times, but I think that was from growing up the way he did. Coming from that family, Elby was used to getting his way."

The way she said *that family* deserved a follow-up, but Mary Ann's text said Jessie had a fever of 102.8. I had to blow out of here.

"Thank you for your time. We'll be in touch."

I stood and looked at Derrick, who was still seated. "We have to get back."

On the way to the front door, I said to Baylor, "This is the first time I've been back here. I like it; it's really nice. How long have you been here?"

"I was one of the first in here, about three years now."

She had lied about who had paid for the place. If the divorce was finalized thirteen months ago, she wouldn't have had the money to buy her new home. The money had to have come from somewhere, and what better place than your rich boyfriend?

Maybe she was concerned she'd lose the house, or it could be something more troubling. Lies were like mosquitoes: if there was one, you could be sure there were others on the way.

# 7

Before I closed the Cherokee's door, Derrick said, "What was that?"

"Jessie's sick. She has a high fever. Mary Ann took her to the doctor."

"Oh no. How high?"

"Almost a hundred and three."

"I know it's scary, but kids run high fevers. You remember my nephew, right? He had a hundred and five a couple of times."

"A hundred and three is high, man."

"You want me to drop you off, meet Mary Ann at the doctor?"

"That'd be great. It's close by, next to NCH on Immokalee."

"No problem. What did you think about Baylor?"

"She lied about using the divorce proceeds to pay for most of the house."

"You'd think she'd have a little shame going out with a married man for four years."

Derrick was moving up the godparent ladder. "I'm not

condoning it, but it takes two to tango, and it seems Elby liked to dance."

"We should take a look at her husband. He could have been involved."

"No question he needs to be cleared, but why wait so long? They had a four-year relationship."

"Maybe something happened recently to push him over the edge. Maybe the reality of losing his wife sank in. He starts drinking, gets dark."

"Sounds like a TV show you're cooking up."

"Real life is stranger than the crap they put on the tube."

"No doubt. We'll see her again, after the brother. It may be that he knows something about the husband's reaction."

Derrick pulled in front of the doctor's building. "Good luck, I'm sure she's going to be fine."

"Thanks."

"Let me know what's going on with her as soon as you know, okay?"

I burst through the building's glass doors and took the steps two at a time to the third floor. Mary Ann was coming out of Dr. Amato's office.

"How is she?"

"Ear infection."

Jessie was sleeping. "She's all flushed."

"You should have seen her before the doctor gave her some baby Tylenol. Doctor Amato said to keep an eye on it and give her more if the fever flares up. She sent a prescription for amoxicillin to CVS."

"Let's get her home, and I'll go pick it up."

I sent a text to Derrick telling him Jessica was doing better and to pick me up at my house.

I STARED at the address for Chadwick Salter. Really? I tried to figure out why Annabelle didn't tell me that he lived next door, on the same property. Was it a purposeful omission? Or a harmless oversight?

The victim's brother was cordial over the phone but wanted to meet at his office on Route 41. Two Salter interviews, and I wouldn't get a glimpse into either of their homes. Was that orchestrated? Or were they that private?

Chadwick's office was on the second floor of a building painted sky blue and pink. It was freshly painted and maintained but dated. It was probably built in the seventies. I looked for an elevator or lobby. There weren't any. Stairs led to hallways that ran across the front and rear of the building for access to the various offices. This place may have been put up in the fifties.

Walking along the rear corridor, I scanned the parking lot. Nothing expensive stood out. The sign on the door for Suite 208 read, *Southern Enterprises*. This wasn't low profile; it bordered on invisible.

There were two rows, four desks each, and a pair of offices behind them. Chadwick was in the one without a window that offered a view of the tiled office space. He stood as I was shown in. His office had a rug, but it wasn't new or plush. One wall had several pictures of Chadwick and his golf buddies. Two other pictures included Elby and the same men fishing off a large boat.

Chadwick Salter was four years younger than his brother. Sandy haired and blue-eyed, Chadwick had a square jaw. He was lean but not skinny. There was a small scar above his right eyebrow.

"My condolences on the loss of your brother."

His deep voice took me by surprise.

"Thank you. It's left a substantial void in my heart and life. I don't believe it will ever be filled."

"Sorry, it must be tough. I assume you were close with your brother."

"Elby was my older brother. We had our ups and downs growing up, but he was my protector."

Protector? From what?

"Just the two of you?"

He exhaled. "Yeah, just Elby and me."

"I know it's small consolation, but I'm going to do my best to find who killed him."

Chadwick silently pawed his chin.

"Since you were close, maybe you have an idea on who might have done this."

"Not really."

"Not really? Tell me what you're thinking."

"No, it's nothing."

"The tiniest of clues are helpful. What did you want to share?"

"It's probably nothing, but Elby, he liked women and had several girlfriends over the years. I didn't approve of it. He was married, after all. I told him all the time it was danger-ous, especially with women who were married. Plus, you have all the sexually transmitted diseases out there. You don't want to bring that home."

"Are you married?"

"Yes, fifteen years now."

"We've talked with Cindy Baylor already. Is there anyone else he was seeing that we should speak with?"

"You spoke to Cindy already?"

"Yes. Why?"

"Well, she was married when Elby started up with her. I can tell you her husband wasn't amused by the affair."

"Was there any indication that he wanted revenge?"

"I don't know anything personally, but Elby had mentioned that he was steamed up."

I wondered how he would characterize a killer's actions.

"We'll take a look into that. You and Elby were business partners, correct?"

"To a certain degree."

"Could you elaborate?"

"We've been fortunate to be part of a family that has made, and continues to make, investments in the state of Florida. The investment vehicle for a majority of the family's holdings are trusts."

"What kinds of investments?"

"They are varied but geared toward a greater good, helping to build a state with a proper infrastructure to support sustainable, growing businesses, and recreation opportunities to facilitate a healthy, happy populace."

He wasn't in politics, but he should be. "That's a big-picture goal."

"Daddy always said to dream big, set goals, and then take action."

"Solid advice. I know the family owns car dealerships throughout the state, but what other businesses are there?"

"We're a private family, Detective Luca, and these are privately held businesses."

"I'm trying to understand if there is a connection between any business interests and the person or persons who killed your brother."

"And I appreciate your efforts in that regard."

"And what about the businesses outside of the trust? Were you and your brother partners in them?"

"No."

"Okay. Did he have other partners?"

"The family had a rule, and Daddy adhered to it. Ninety percent of our investments were as a family. However, he wanted to foster creativity and risk-taking by allowing each of us to go it alone or with partners of our choosing. But the rule was a maximum ten percent."

A rule? "How did that rule get enforced?"

"If you must know, it is codified in the trust."

Another case of somebody controlling things from the grave. "Tell me something about your brother's solo ventures. What kinds of businesses, and did he have partners?"

"Elby wasn't as disciplined on his own deals as he had to be with the family's investments."

"So, he made mistakes in businesses?"

He nodded. "He was stubborn. I tried to caution him, but he said he had his own mind and would invest in what, and with who, he wanted to."

"Did that upset your family?"

"Of course, not the investments, but at times the people he associated with."

"Would they be the type of people we'd call gangsters?"

He snorted. "Don't be ridiculous."

"Then what were you referring to?"

"I'd prefer not to say. No matter how I expressed it, it wouldn't sound nice."

"Would it be breeding? People from different classes of society?"

A hint of a smile surfaced. I had my answer and wasn't surprised by it.

"Everybody has to come from somewhere. Now, I'm going to need to have an understanding of what your brother's business interests were and who any partners may have been."

"I'll have to speak to our attorneys about what must be disclosed."

"That's fair enough. But I'll need access as fast as possible."

"I understand. As soon as the family consults, you'll receive a call. It shouldn't be any later than tomorrow."

**8**

────────

FEELING THE PAIN IN MY GUT, I PUT THE GROCERY BAG ON the counter.

"Where is she?"

"She's napping."

"Does she have a fever?"

Mary Ann put the milk in the fridge. "I told you two hours ago, Frank, no."

"I know, but these ear infections can come back. I told you about all the trouble I had with them growing up."

"She's going to be fine."

"I hope she didn't inherit whatever defective gene I had that made me get one infection after another. Remember, I told you, my speech was getting affected, and my mom took me to a healing mass?"

"How could I forget? It was a miracle you were cured by that priest."

"Do you think stuff like that gets passed down?"

"I don't know. I guess it's possible, but there's nothing we can do about it."

"We have to keep an eye on it. Take her temperature daily or something."

She put down the head of cauliflower she was holding. "What's going on, Frank?"

"Nothing. I'm just worried about Jessie, that's all."

"She had an ear infection. Every baby ever born has had them."

"I know, but this gene thing had me thinking . . ."

"About cancer? Is that what you're concerned about?"

"Yeah. Remember Croce in Financial Crimes? His wife had lung cancer, so did her mother, grandmother, and sister."

"I think it depends. I know they have gene therapies to treat certain cancers, but they're not all passed down. If they were, you'd see it. I really don't think we have to worry about her getting bladder cancer."

"Maybe we should ask the doctor. See what she says."

"Sure. There are all kinds of tests these days. If she thinks Jessica needs to be tested, we'll do it."

"That's a good idea."

"I have to get dinner going before she wakes up, but we never talked about her christening."

"It's just that I think we shouldn't wait, that's all. Anything can happen."

"You're turning into a worrywart. Nothing's going to happen to Jessica."

"I know, but . . ."

"If it makes you happy, I'll call St. Agnes in the morning and see what their schedule looks like."

"Good, I don't think it's a problem. Nowadays, they baptize ten babies at a time."

"I hope there's not too many when we do it. It doesn't feel as special when there's a crowd."

"The important thing is to get her baptized."

"We have to make a decision on the godparents. But I'm not doing it now; we have to eat before Jessica gets up."

That wasn't a problem for me. I wanted to take a leak. The pain I felt when I came in had dulled considerably, and I was hoping that relieving myself would make it disappear. I had two more days until my doctor visit.

INSTEAD OF GOING to see Ron Weaver, who'd taken a trip to Arizona, I was going to see Cindy Baylor's ex-husband. Fred Baylor owned an agency that handled claims adjusting for auto insurers. He was located in a building just off Fifth Avenue.

There were a handful of smokers standing outside the building getting their dose of nicotine, every one of them glued to their phones. What was driving society's need to seek instant answers to meaningless questions?

There were a dozen desks in the main office area, each manned by workers wearing headsets. It was a busy place, generating enough money to pay for a hit man.

The sign on Fred Baylor's office door read *Claims Adjuster Manager*. It was no-frills office with a metal desk and cheap artwork, but there was a nice view out the window. He was on the phone but stood when I was shown in. Six foot, muscular, with a crew cut—had he been in the Marine Corp?

"Sorry, that was one of our better clients."

"No problem. It sure is busy here."

"No shortage of fender benders in this town. Between tourists who don't know where they're going, cell phones, and a lot of eighty-year-old drivers, we keep busy."

"I wanted to ask you about Elby Salter."

"I saw what happened to him in the paper."

"Your ex-wife and he were in a relationship. What do you know about it?"

"What's that supposed to mean? Of course I wasn't happy about it, but I didn't go out and kill him."

"Did you ever threaten him?"

"No."

"We have a witness who said that you did threaten Elby Salter, telling him to stay away from your wife, or he'd regret it."

"Look, are you married?"

"That has nothing to do with this case."

"Yeah, well, you have some rich dude come and take your wife away from you. What was I supposed to do, just sit there? I didn't know what to do. I confronted Cindy, but it didn't work."

"So, you tried to scare away Salter with threats?"

He shrugged. "I didn't know what to do. I knew Cindy was partly to blame, but this guy, he had money and was throwing it at her. You know, he bought that Mercato place for her."

"We know about that. But it's not a crime."

"Well, it should be. He used shit like that to steal my wife. It's like offering a kid candy to take a ride with some pedophile."

It wasn't, but arguing the point was like trying to explain America to a radical Islamic cleric.

"If you did anything else to intimidate Elby Salter, tell me now. We'll find out anyway, so you may as well tell me now."

He looked me in the eyes and held them. "I just wanted my wife back, that's all. I made some threats, but I never followed through or anything. You know, Salter's done this before. There are plenty of husbands pissed at the bastard."

Fred Baylor wasn't being completely honest. He needed another look, but it didn't feel like he was the killer.

---

DERRICK WAS GLUED to his monitor. "How'd it go with the girlfriend's ex-husband?"

"He's hiding something. He admitted to trying to scare Salter, but I don't think he's our guy."

"Why you say that?"

"Just a feeling at this point. We're going to have to dig deeper into him if we don't have anything else."

"We don't. I'm going over the report from forensics on the crime scene."

"Don't tell me there's nothing."

"Zippo. Two of the hairs found on Salter's body were not his, but they ran them through the DNA system, and no matches came up."

"Damn. Did they run it against the national data bank?"

"Yep. But you never know, the rate at which DNA is being added to the system . . ."

"The entire country should do what Florida just started doing the first of the year."

"You mean the new law that went into effect?"

"Exactly. You get arrested, you get swabbed for DNA, and it goes into the data bank."

"I never understood how it was different from getting fingerprinted when you were arrested."

"Some of this privacy crap is plain stupid. When you get hauled in, we take mug shots, fingerprint you, and create a record of it all. Years ago, pictures were taken to identify people. As methodology improved, they started taking finger-prints. Collecting DNA is just a natural extension."

"There's a couple of states that did it before Florida did. I bet in a couple of years every state will be doing it."

"Maybe we'll finally get an easy one to solve, then."

"It'd be nice to have an automated system for DNA in cold cases to check against the new samples that come in."

"I'll be long retired by that time, if it ever comes to that."

"How much longer do you think you'll be doing this?"

"I used to say until I dropped dead. Tracking down killers is what makes me tick, but I got to say, being a father and all, I have to make sure I'm around for Jessie. A couple more nuts like Dwyer come after me, I'm going to rethink it. I owe it to my family."

## 9

Chadwick was true to his word. We had an appointment with a lawyer who represented the family. Unfortunately, it was an attorney who represented many of the ultra wealthy. It's not that Peter Gerey was a bad guy, it was the fact he was good at protecting his clients. To him, privacy was more sacred than life itself.

He represented the Boggs one of the wealthiest families in Naples, in a case I worked two years ago. He never violated any protocols but never offered anything. He shielded the Boggs so well I had a mental image of him as a legal version of Superman: chest out, hands on his hips, clients behind an impenetrable wall. He'd make a good guardian for Jessica.

White, Gerey and Blackburn occupied a two-story, white stucco building just north of Golden Gate. Tucked in the corner of a small parking lot that served two other buildings, you needed a microscope to see their sign. A pair of late-model Mercedes framed the single door of their offices.

Derrick said, "You were right; this place is almost invisible. Most of the high-profile attorneys I've run into have fancy offices."

"That's just it. Most of Gerey's clients want to fly under the radar."

I hit the call button, and we were buzzed in.

Gerey was seated in a far corner, signing documents at a round table when we entered. He penned a couple more before rising to greet us, shoeing away a secretary who had started toward us. He had aged noticeably in the last two years. Had he gotten sick, or was it the pressure of safeguarding his clients that took a toll? We shook hands.

"It's good to see you, Detective Luca."

"Same here, Counselor. This is my partner, Detective Derrick Dickson."

"Nice to meet you."

"Likewise."

"I heard you had married your former partner and now have a child. Is that right?"

"Yes. Been looking into my personal life, Counselor?"

"No. It just came up when we were gathering the data you requested. How are you enjoying fatherhood?"

"It's been great."

"Excellent. Let's step into my office."

Gerey's office was done in a dark paneled wood that looked like walnut. Heavy drapes shut out most of the light. Gerey slid behind an oversized desk, and Derrick and I took seats in leather wing chairs.

"Would you care for something to drink, gentlemen?"

We declined.

"I understand your interest in the late Elby Salter's business holdings. These are private businesses, and their activities are unrelated to the death of Mr. Salter."

"We don't know that. We're conducting an investigation into his murder, and his business interests may or may not have anything to do with it."

"The holdings are expansive, and on the remote chance that there is a connection, it would purely relate to one entity. We cannot allow a myriad of activities to be disrupted or reputations tarnished by your investigation."

Derrick said, "Mr. Gerey, you have our commitment that we'll be discreet in checking the possibility that Mr. Salter's murder was business related."

"While your personal assurance is welcome and appreciated, I have counseled the family on a reasonable approach. We are firm in our belief that the sensible route is a limited one. We'll release information incrementally. That will ensure the family's privacy is compromised in a controlled way."

I said, "Counselor, we're investigating a homicide, the death of a Salter family member. We're not about to go hog wild, but we will not be stonewalled when we believe there is a trail to pursue."

"Detective Luca, rest assured the family's primary interest is their safety. They want the perpetrator of this heinous crime brought to justice and will cooperate, in a controlled and reasonable manner, to accomplish that."

"That's good, Counselor, but we can't agree to being spoon-fed information. It will hamper our investigation."

"I am willing to assist you, but you must understand my hands are tied."

Derrick put his hand on my arm. He knew I was about to tell him I'd go around his stonewalling ass. Derrick said, "We understand your concerns, Mr. Gerey. Release the information you are comfortable with, and we'll get on our way."

Gerey's face relaxed, then quickly tightened. He was used to winning, but not that fast. He paused before opening a drawer and taking a folder out.

"I prepared a listed of holdings, limited to entities that have no family members as partners." He slid the folder across the desk. "In the spirit of cooperation, I took the liberty of including a couple of ventures that failed as well."

The Salter family didn't have the Midas touch after all. I opened the folder. A single sheet of paper was all it contained. There were ten businesses listed. Gerey considered this a limited list? How many businesses were there?

My eyes drifted to the bottom three. They were annotated *Ceased Operations*. The last one, Power Supplements Ltd., had closed just a month ago. A name that I was vaguely familiar with was listed as a partner. It felt like we had something to work with.

We hopped in the Cherokee and I said, "You handled yourself like a pro. These attorneys can be so damn smug."

Derrick pulled onto Route 41. "I just figured whatever he gave us would give us a starting point."

"You're right. Gerey's going to protect his clients, but I don't think he'd hide anything connected with a homicide, unless the family had something to do with it."

"I can't see that."

"At this point I can't either, but I don't need to remind you that when lions have to, they eat their own cubs."

"I thought that was a myth."

"Nope. When food is scare, a lion will eat its cubs to survive. Humans don't do it for food, extremely rare occasions excepted; they do it to protect themselves, to keep a secret, secret. But enough on that. There's a company on here that shut down a month ago. The partner is Robert Freidman. It rings a bell, but I can't place it."

"Isn't that the guy who did those infomercials?"

"Shit, you're right. There were a bunch of allegations that they weren't shipping the same products they advertised, right?"

"I don't remember exactly, but he seemed like a shyster to me."

"Maybe Gerey wasn't giving us a hard time after all. There had to be a reason he put companies that are closed on the list. He may be trying to send a signal."

# 10

FRIEDMAN WAS A MEMBER OF THE QUAIL CREEK COUNTRY Club and wanted to meet there. I was surprised by how active the clubhouse was. There were two valet kids for the cars and a long line of golf carts bordering the driveway.

The clubhouse restaurant looked full. My mouth watered from the aroma of roasting meat. The hostess pointed out Robert Friedman sitting by a window, in a white sweater, reading a newspaper. I passed a row of carving stations and rapped a knuckle on his table. We shook hands, and I sat down.

Robert Friedman was one of those men who'd had work done on his face, attempting to preserve a youthful look. I'm not passing judgment, but what was puzzling was he took enough sun to have a deep tan. Another contradiction was his hair and mustache. They were four shades too dark for his sixty-seven years on the planet. Didn't he, and countless other men, see it looked unnatural, actually exposing their age?

It was early in the game for me, but I hoped I'd have the sense to age as gracefully as my ego would allow. I'm sure, as the years piled up, a tug-of-war would ensue. I was already late to the fatherhood scene, and I wouldn't want Jessie to worry her dad was older than the other kids' parents.

"This is one busy place."

"This your first time here?"

"Yes."

"It's a very active club. Most members don't even live here. The staff is wonderful. The golfing is great, and they always talk about the tennis program. They just hired the pro from Pelican Marsh, I hear."

"How long have you been a member?"

"At least ten years. I used to belong to Imperial, but it was too highbrow there for me, if you know what I mean."

A waitress came over, and Friedman ordered a gin and tonic. I asked for a Diet Coke.

"The Imperial Club, is that where you met Elby Salter?"

"I didn't know Elby was a member there."

Neither did I. "Where did you meet him?"

"We met through John Heights, a friend of mine who was friends with Ron Weaver. As you probably know, Ronnie and Elby are, uh, were, good friends."

"John Heights? Don't think I know the name."

"He runs strength programs for a couple of major league teams, and I know he was also involved with the Cowboys at one time."

"Did he create any of those weight-loss, muscle-builder things you were selling on TV?"

He moved the newspaper off the table onto a chair. "We carried a lot of products that were well received."

The waitress delivered our drinks. "Here you are, Mr. Friedman. Are you boys ready to order?"

Friedman said, "I'll have the tuna salad. Tell Andre to go light on the dressing."

"Absolutely. And you, sir?"

"A burger, medium rare."

"Fries or fruit?"

"Uh, I'll have the fries, but don't tell my wife."

"No worries, sir. I hope you don't mind, but you know, you look like George Clooney."

"I've heard that before. Thanks."

The waitress left and Friedman said, "The kid is right. You do look like him."

"It'd be nice to have his money. Now, tell me about Power Supplements Ltd. You and Elby Salter were partners in it. How did you come to go into business together?"

"The nutritional supplement business is a huge industry. Last year, there were over a hundred and thirty billion dollars in sales, and it's growing at almost ten percent per year. Elby liked the size and growth of the marketplace. Also, the fact that it is largely unregulated was attractive to him."

"What was Power Supplements?"

"Well, we had visions of an integrated company. We'd focus on catching the newest wave and tweak a product, getting it to market ahead of the major players."

"You're losing me."

"Let's take something like calcium supplements. Most are not differentiated except the size of the dose. What we were doing was adding an emerging benefit. Something like a mushroom extract that has neurological benefits."

That sounded like a multivitamin to me. "So, someone would take one pill and get two benefits."

"Exactly. There's a limit to how many pills people want to take. But the key was using evolving medicinal practices, introducing cutting-edge therapeutic compounds before they became mainstream."

"Oh, you had people researching new compounds . . ."

"No. There's plenty of researching going on. There's no

reason to duplicate those efforts. We wanted to be the company that brought them to the people first. It was all about speed to market."

"I get it. What happened?"

"Well, we got off to a decent start. We caught the big boys sitting on their asses. They woke up and jumped in. They came in quicker than our business plan provided for. We knew they'd come in eventually, but we believed we'd have our own production facilities operating at the time."

"You outsourced the production?"

"We had an edge. We couldn't wait to build facilities; it would take too long. We'd lose our advantage. We had lined up enough production capacity to get us through two years before our plant would be built. It cost us more, and we were losing money as a result, but Elby knew that until we had our own factories we'd operate in the red."

"What happened?"

"He had two pieces of property in Collier: one out in Harker off Twenty-Nine, the other in Sunniland, and a backup plot in Lee County, just past Lehigh Acres, reserved for manufacturing facilities. We filed plans, and they got kicked back eight or nine times. We lost a year screwing around with engineers and architects trying to get approval. It was frustrating as hell. Collier rejected it, even though we would create two hundred high-paying jobs. They claimed they had concerns about chemical runoffs. We decided to build in Lee and started the process all over."

"How long was this now?"

"Eighteen to twenty months."

"And you were losing money every month?"

He nodded. "A hundred fifty grand a month, plus all the money we were spending on consultants, engineers, and goddamn lawyers. But Elby didn't seem to mind in the beginning. He has deep pockets, as you know. Plus, we had a business plan. We drew it up together. It showed we'd lose three to four million before we built our own. We were actually ahead of schedule, not by much, but ahead."

"Mr. Salter pulled the plug?"

He nodded. "He went from hot to cold, like a frigging faucet. He wouldn't reason with me; you couldn't talk to him. Look, I didn't put up what he did, but I had half a million in it."

"Did he lose interest? Or felt the plan you had drawn wasn't going to work?"

"It would have worked. I showed it to a bunch of people, investors and all. You know, I have a couple of people I'm talking with that are interested in going forward. Just not down here."

"In Florida?"

"No, the state is fine, just not Southwest Florida. One of my guys is interested. He has pull in Alabama and believes we'd even get tax credits to help us build there. He guarantees there wouldn't be any issues getting permits."

"What changed Mr. Salter's mind?"

"I wish I knew. Like I said, we were on plan, and in a snap he was out."

"That must have been upsetting."

"Damn right it was. The fucker, uh, sorry, it was confusing. We were on track, and I believed in it. You know?"

What I knew was we had to look into what flipped Elby's switch. Was it something he learned about Friedman? Or something else? Or simply a rich guy's boredom?

I finished up my burger, which may have been the reason the restaurant was so busy, and left. On the way to my car, a text came in from Derrick: *Call me when you can. We got something!*

**11**

———

Thinking over what Derrick told me had percolated a line of ideas. As soon as I stepped into the office, I told him, "The first thing we have to do is check whatever video feed there is."

"I checked with the Chase branch. It's an outside drive-up ATM. I asked Sanchez to go down and grab the video."

"The three-thousand-dollar withdrawal doesn't make sense. I never heard of a limit so high. I'm limited to, I think, eight hundred a day in withdrawals."

"Mine is capped at a thousand."

"Call the bank, ask the manager about it. There might be something to this."

"You think it was a robbery? Forced him to withdraw the money at an ATM and then killed him? Like a carjacking gone wrong? Or an addict that panicked?"

"I don't think so. This was no panic; this was planned. His hands bound, shot in the back of the head and dumped."

"You're right, a druggie might kill for three grand, but he wouldn't do it that way."

"If it wasn't a forced withdrawal, then what did he need

three thousand for? That's a lot of money, even for someone with his means."

"Everyone uses credit cards, PayPal, or checks. Cash is going extinct."

"Except when you want to hide or save the tax on something. But sales tax on three grand is a hundred and eighty bucks. I don't think he needs to save that."

"You'd be surprised, Frank. Some of the richest people are the cheapest."

"That's how they got rich in the first place."

"Don't spend more than you make. It works for everyone."

No one was going to knock Derrick off the top of the guardian ladder.

"Amen. Let's kick this around. Why would he need that much cash? The obvious answer is to buy drugs."

"You think he was doing drugs?"

"The fact is, I never thought to ask anybody we talked to. We need to follow that up."

"I'll touch base with his wife, girlfriend, and brother."

"Thanks. Now, the autopsy didn't evidence the presence of illicit drugs in Elby's system. If he were using, it wasn't before he was murdered. Maybe he was making a buy or providing the cash to a girlfriend to buy."

"Maybe he was buying a piece of jewelry for a woman and didn't want to leave a trail."

"Annabelle doesn't strike me like the type of woman who'd pore over credit card bills. They probably have a family office that handles all their bills. Why don't we let this percolate and follow up with the bank and the drug use angle?"

"Sounds good."

"Maybe later today or tomorrow I'd like to talk to you about something, something personal."

"Sure, Frank. Whenever you like."

"It's nothing bad; it's all good. Let's get to work."

---

THE WITHDRAWAL WAS MADE at 5:43 p.m. at the Chase branch in Estero, off Corkscrew Road. Assuming someone hadn't forced him to go to an ATM, I wondered whether Elby Salter was heading north for his meeting in Fort Myers, or did something else bring him to the corner of Tamiami Trail and Corkscrew Road?

Derrick inserted the thumb drive from the bank. I wanted to see if there was anything suspicious going on before the withdrawal and told him to fast-forward to a time stamp of 5:20.

He hit play. "Here we go."

For a drive-up ATM, the pictures were clear. We watched nine cars come into the ATM lane and complete transactions. Out of habit, I jotted down license plate numbers as 5:43 approached.

A white Ford Explorer, matching the one registered to Elby Salter, came into view.

"Freeze it, and check the plate number."

Derrick stopped the tape and checked the numbers. "It's his."

"It looks like there's someone in the passenger seat."

The SUV waited behind a Porsche 911. As soon as the sports car finished its transaction, Elby Salter's car pulled along the ATM. Elby was behind the wheel. He pivoted toward the cash machine. He slid his card in. I'd never met him, but his facial features didn't appear stressed.

He punched the keyboard a couple of times and looked both ways. A few seconds later he reached for his card, and then the cash. He didn't request a receipt, which I found odd. But before he drove off he reached out and wiped his fingers across the keyboard.

"Pause it. Right there, he's smearing his fingertips across the keys just in case someone is either reading his finger movements or wants to trace his finger oils."

"It's not an ATM-jack."

"That's right."

"So, whoever killed him got a bonus they probably didn't expect."

"If it was a contracted kill, they told him to take any money and ID to make it look like a robbery. But with three grand, I'm sure he'd keep that part quiet. Hit play."

As the Explorer pulled away, I said, "It looks like someone might be in the passenger seat."

"I don't know. If so, it doesn't look like it would be a man. Maybe a kid or a woman."

"Headrests are too damn big these days. Run it again, in slow-mo."

We watched it two more times but couldn't pick anything else up. What we learned was it wasn't a forced withdrawal, a time and place where Elby was, and a little bit about him. He was cautious, at least with money. Elby had looked around as the transaction was unfolding, and he tried to prevent anyone from reading his pin number.

―――――

## 12

"Morning, Frank. I spoke with the manager over at Chase. He said Salter had a five-thousand-dollar limit, per day."

I picked up the coffee Derrick always brought me. "Five grand? That's a lot of cash." I took a sip, and it was perfect.

"I know."

"Well, he didn't go for the limit. I'll have to think over whatever that might mean."

"Annabelle Salter called me back this morning."

I looked at my watch. It was only eight forty-five. "Already?"

"Yep, called at eight thirty on the button."

"You've been busy this morning."

"She claimed to not know if Elby was doing any drugs."

"That means no to me. A man's wife would know if he were on drugs, just like she knew he was screwing around on her."

"Unless he did it only with his girlfriend."

"Remote possibility. I know there are a lot of people who

claim to be recreational users, but their definition of recreational is a lot wider than mine."

"Maybe the cash was for a buy for his girlfriend."

"Could be. Annabelle called at eight thirty?"

"Yeah, that's what I said."

"Why? That's early in anyone's book. That seems like an attempt to prove she's cooperative."

"It could be genuine, Frank. It *was* her husband."

"We need to know about any life insurance she may be the beneficiary of and what any prenuptial looked like. Was there a financial benefit to having her husband killed?"

"You think it was her?"

"I'm not making judgments; I'm exploring possibilities."

"Who we going to ask? Their lawyer?"

"No, let's start with Chadwick. He may give us something, but before we go, I want to talk to you."

"Sure, what's up?"

I closed the door to our office.

"Mary Ann and I talked it over last night, and we'd like to ask you if you would like to be Jessica's godfather."

"What? Oh my gosh. Of course. It would be an honor."

He got up and wrapped his arms around me.

"Great." I wriggled free. "We're not settled on a godmother just yet, but we're planning on having the christening at St. Agnes in three weeks."

"Oh. What do I have to do?"

"There's some paperwork from the church. I'll bring it in tomorrow. I just wanted to make sure you were okay with it."

"I'm more than okay." He squeezed my shoulder. "It's a privilege. I love Jessica, and I'll be the best godfather I can, Frank."

"I know you will, that's why I wanted you. She is going

to need the support of good people like you during her life. Parents can't do it all."

---

"TURN IN HERE; that's the building."

"This is where Chadwick Salter has his office?"

"Like I said before, the wealthy get that way by keeping an eye on what goes out the door."

Derrick pulled into a space. "But they're way beyond wealthy. They could burn hundred-dollar bills when they need heat in January."

"They're a legacy family. No one born into that family has to work, but it looks like there are requirements to do something, not just sit on your ass. I liked the way Warren Buffet said it, something like giving his kids enough money, so they could do anything but not enough so they could do nothing."

"That's a great way to put it."

Walking around the back of the building, I said, "We're not in these guys' league, but we're not going to spoil Jessie. She wants something, it's not going to be an automatic. I remember I wanted a minibike like all the other kids had, but even though my dad could have bought one he said no. If I wanted one, I had to work for it. Guess what? I was delivering newspapers the following week."

"Your father had some wisdom."

"Look, something happens to me and Mary Ann, don't go spoiling Jessica, even though you feel sorry for her."

"What are you talking about, Frank? You're not going anywhere."

"Let's hope so."

"There's no elevator?"

"Nope."

The office was busier than on my last visit. Chadwick was standing in the doorway of his office talking to an older man. His shoulders sagged when he saw us. We waited for him as the smell of coffee brewing filled the office. I could use a cup, and if the offer came, I was going to have one.

The gray-haired man headed toward us, and Chadwick retreated to his office. We were about to be brushed off with a manufactured conflict. Stripping off his glasses, this man looked like he was used to shooing away solicitors.

"Mr. Salter is extremely busy, gentlemen, but he has a couple of minutes to spare. So, please keep it short."

Derrick said, "Absolutely."

"Good. Go on back, he's waiting."

Chadwick stood and greeted us. His Barry White voice still surprised me. Anyone talking to him on the phone would never picture him in person.

Derrick said, "Thank you for squeezing us in. We have a couple of quick questions."

"Anything I can do to help."

There was no offer of coffee. I said, "Did your brother do drugs?"

"No. I don't believe so."

"Did he ever use drugs as a teenager?"

"He smoked a little marijuana way back, but who didn't? Elby liked his vodka growing up, usually with cranberry. He still drinks it, albeit with diet cranberry juice these days."

His smile faded when I asked, "I assume your brother had substantial life insurance coverage. Who was the beneficiary?"

"That's a private matter."

"It's a possible motivating factor. Who would benefit from his death?"

"I am unaware if Elby had additional policies, but family protocol requires proceeds from insurance on the lives of those who came into the world as Salters to benefit the Salter family trust."

I noticed that Chadwick had not looked at his watch once.

Derrick said, "Understood. But concerning the distinction from those born as Salters and those who marry into the family, does that mean that someone like Annabelle would not be a beneficiary of the trust?"

"Gentlemen, again we are delving into areas that virtually anyone would agree are private. All I am willing to say, at this point, is that ample provisions are made for a spouse upon death or divorce."

"Did your brother and his wife have a prenuptial agreement?"

"Yes."

Remembering a previous case involving a wealthy family who used the same attorney, I said, "I assume that the trust requires one in order to draw benefits. Is that correct?"

"Yes."

I was curious about the children Salter women birthed. If they took the father's name, they wouldn't come into the world as Salters. I wanted to ask, but knew they had that figured out. Instead, I asked, "I understand the privacy aspect and respect that, but could you at least give us an indication of what a spouse would receive upon a divorce from or death of a Salter?"

"Let's just say something to supplement a middle-class existence. They'd have to provide for themselves, but a certain safety net would be there."

"Regardless of a long, happy marriage?"

"Elby's marriage was neither long nor happy."

Derrick said, "How well did you know Cindy Baylor?"

"I know of Ms. Baylor."

"Enough to know if she were using drugs?"

"There seems to be a preoccupation with the use of drugs. Is there something I should know?"

"We're asking the questions here, Mr. Salter. Do you have any knowledge of Ms. Baylor using drugs?"

"No. Gentlemen, I wish I had more time for you, but I must go. I have an appointment in twenty minutes and cannot be late."

We left the office, and walking down the outside corridor to the stairs, Derrick said, "Sorry, I shouldn't have made that comment about who's asking the questions."

"Doesn't matter. We got a lot of info."

"Guess the wife is off the hook if she isn't going to get a big payday."

Going down the stairs, I said, "Something about Chadwick rubs me the wrong way. I can't put my finger on it yet. I'd like to wait in the parking lot and see if he really has an appointment."

"You want to?"

"Nah, what would it prove? We came unannounced. He may not have an appointment, but I'm sure he has things to do, like we do."

**13**

———

Huge iron gates swung open, and I entered Talis Park. It was about as high-end a community as you'd find. I'd heard it was even more exclusive before the developer went belly-up, and they had to put a bunch of low-rise buildings and coach homes in to make the math work.

I waited for the paver entrance to end, but it fed into a main drag that was also made of pavers. Passing a large lake, a bridge that Tuscany would be proud of came into view. I drove over the bridge into a circular green space anchored by a Washington Memorial-like obelisk.

The sign for valet parking was straight ahead. I circled around, looking for parking and squeezed into a spot even though it said *Golf Carts Only*. I couldn't stand tipping a kid when a parking space was steps away. A buck or two is okay, but nowadays, five bucks was expected, minimum. I was a cop, not an investment banker.

An elegant lobby fed into an understated courtyard, leading to the dining facilities that were small by Naples standards but nicely done. There wasn't a seat at the bar. I scanned the room, and a woman approached me, directing me to an outdoor patio where my date was.

I recognized him from the pictures I'd seen, and waved. Ronald Weaver rose out of his seat and moved like the athlete he once was. He was fifty-two but had maintained a boyish figure. Six foot and change, Weaver's brown hair was thinning, but he was slim, and his golf shirt hugged his biceps, making him look like he was in his early forties.

His hand enveloped mine. I liked it when a man looked me in the eye when we shook hands.

"Say, I'm really sorry I was out in Phoenix. I wouldn't have gone if I knew what was happening with Elby."

"I understand. No problem."

"You want something to drink. How about a brew?"

I coveted the half-eaten hamburger on his plate. "A Diet Coke please."

"You got it."

I surveyed the view. There was a difference in the color of the greens and fairways. It looked like it was manicured with scissors. To the right, homes as large as the clubhouse lined a gated street. Beverly Hills would be jealous.

"I could get used to this view. It's the first time I've been in here."

"I'm one of the original settlers here. If you ever want to play a round of golf, let me know."

"Sounds good, but I don't play."

"It's better that way. The game can be frustrating as hell."

"How'd you land in here?"

"It always attracted athletes. One of the original guys in here was Rocco Mediate, a pro golfer, and a couple of guys from the Sox bought homes in here."

"I understand Elby Salter was a big Red Sox fan."

"Oh yeah. Huge. We went to the game the day he went missing."

"Were you with him the entire time?"

A waitress poured my Coke out of the can into a glass.

"Not the whole time. We both knew a bunch of people, and you know, you move around during the game, bullshitting to this one or that one."

"Did you go to the game together?"

"No. Elby met me up there. I still work for the team, really scouting, that's why I was in Phoenix, for the Sox."

"I heard you were the general manager."

"Nah, my title is assistant GM, but the team has two other ones. I'm a talent guy, evaluate the players. Make recommendations on who to sign. It's a lot more complicated than it used to be. It's not just the ability of the player. Now we have to balance what they get paid."

"I'm just curious, were you involved in the Peters decision?"

Weaver rolled his eyes. "Yep, and you'd think I sent somebody's newborn to another country. You can't believe the hate mail we got. It's still coming in. I needed security to get to my car for two weeks.

"Over a player? Some people take this sports thing a bit too far."

"It was an easy call to make. The guy was overpaid; he wanted over twenty million a year. We got this kid, Sanchez, in triple-A; he's something else. I think he'll be ready for the big leagues by the all-star break."

"Sounds promising. When did you get to the stadium that day?"

"I was at the stadium around eleven that morning."

"Did you leave together?"

"No, I had to leave early. I don't know if it was like the

sixth inning or something, I had to check out a kid who plays for the Twins."

"What time was that?"

"It was probably about two thirty or three."

"Did you have lunch together?"

"Nah, we just had a beer and peanuts."

"Elby drank a beer?"

"Not the whole thing. Look, don't take this the wrong way. I loved Elby. We were great friends, but he was different."

"Tell me what you mean."

"He wanted to fit in around here. That's why he made the deal to move the team."

"To fit in?"

"Look, I knew he didn't like beer. He'd have half a glass every time, but instead of saying no, he'd want to be like the rest of the guys. He'd even curse every now and then. Look, it doesn't make him a bad guy. He'd give me the shirt off his back if I asked, and he loved the game. For a kid who played lacrosse or whatever, he knew the ins and outs of baseball."

"Do you have any idea who might have done this? Did Elby have any enemies that you know of?"

Weaver made lines in the condensation forming on his glass. "The short answer is no. But do I have crazy ideas on who might have done it. Yeah, I do."

"Nothing is crazy. Tell me what you're thinking."

"Well, for one, Cindy Baylor is a gold digger, okay. I know that don't make her a murderer, but she was in it for the money."

"But I thought it was a symbiotic relationship. Elby got what he wanted, maybe sex, companionship, and she got some money."

"He'd complain about her, always looking for money for

this or that. He could afford anything, but he didn't like it, that's all. It's probably nothing more than what happens every day around here and a million other places." He spread his arm around.

Much as I would have enjoyed hearing some gossip, I said, "What about her ex-husband?"

"Oh yeah, I almost forgot about him. He went after Elby when Elby started screwing his wife. Elby took it seriously, and even cooled things down with her for a little bit."

"Went after? What did he do?"

"The guy followed Elby around in his car. He was trying to intimidate him. He even came to the stadium one day."

"He was stalking Salter?"

"I guess that's what you'd call it."

"What happened with him?"

"I don't know exactly. Maybe it finally sunk in that his wife was a bitch."

"Maybe."

"You know, talking about stalking, Elby dated this French woman, Marie something or other."

"Redoux?"

"Yeah, that's her. So, you know about her?"

I nodded. "Tell me what you know."

"When Elby broke up with her, she didn't want to let go. She'd hound him, calling him at all hours of the night. She even called Annabelle."

"Did she make any threats that you know of?"

He wagged his head. "No, just that she took the breakup really bad."

"Got it. What about anybody else?"

"Friedman pissed off Elby to no end. I mean, he's another bloodsucker. He hounded Elby to put up the money for the supplement business. The guy was nothing but a con man."

"Did Elby ever say anything about him?"

"Oh yeah, all the time. He was pissed off at the steady stream of bullshit that he'd get from Friedman."

"Is that why he ended up closing the business down?"

"I don't know. Elby never talked much about it. I know he was having some issues with the county, but I'm not sure. I was just glad he was free of that bloodsucker."

"He met Friedman through you, didn't he?"

"No way. Johnny Heights and I were friends, not really tight, but we saw each other around from time to time. He knew Friedman. How he could hang around with Friedman is beyond me. But that's how Elby got hooked up with him."

"Okay. I understand Elby liked to fool around on his wife. What about any other women?"

"His problem was it was always married women. I don't know, maybe it felt safer to him. There was a new woman in the mix. I think her name was Sue. He was going to see her the night I went to Phoenix."

"The day he disappeared?"

"Yeah."

"But Cindy Baylor said she had a date with him that night."

"That's what he told me. Maybe he was going to blow Cindy off."

"And she was married?"

"Yep. As usual."

"And it wasn't his first rendezvous with her?"

"No, he'd seen her before."

"Can you tell me anything else about this woman?"

"I wish I could, but I don't know anything more about her, other than that he seemed too crazy about her."

"Was that unusual?"

"Yeah, Elby was like a high schooler when he told me about her."

"And she was definitely married?"

"Yep. That was his MO."

It was a struggle leaving such a heavenly view, but I had to follow up on what Weaver had told me. Maybe I would take Weaver up on his golf offer one day.

**14**

———

It was the third day in a row that Jessica was sleeping when I came home. I tiptoed for Mary Ann's benefit as I made my way to the bassinet. She was beautiful. I stroked her face and she stirred. I moved her hand, and she opened her eyes. She smiled at me. I reached in and picked her up as Mary Ann came into the room.

"What are you doing?"

"She was up."

"No, she wasn't. I saw you wake her up, on the monitor."

I held her over my head. "Look, she's smiling."

"You're putting her to bed. Good luck."

Mary Ann left the room, and I put Jessie on our bed. I lay down next to her and played with her for a good twenty minutes before putting her back in the bassinet. As I changed out of my work clothes, she began to cry.

I picked her back up, and in five minutes she was sound asleep. I crept out of the bedroom.

"Sleeping like a rock."

"I can't believe it. She never does that."

"What can I tell you? Daddy magic is what it is."

"Yeah, right. Put the grill on."

Waiting for the grill to heat up, I picked up the *Naples Daily News*. There was a picture of three men doing a groundbreaking ceremony for a new hospital in East Naples. They looked familiar, but I couldn't place the faces.

I put the paper down and checked the grill, then it hit me. Those were the same men in the photos in Chadwick Salter's office. I read their names: Robert Hamlet, Michael West, and Marshall Bingham. I read the article. The men were wealthy Naples residents who financed the project on favorable terms because they believed the community needed another medical facility.

It was a feel-good article about members of the community with means stepping up to fill a void when the bankers wanted too much to underwrite the project. I was grateful to live in such a good place to raise Jessie.

---

Cindy Baylor feigned surprise at my visit but had remembered my name. She was wearing jeans, flip-flops, and a white blouse that gave a glimpse of her fine china. She was a female magnet.

"Oh, Detective Luca, is there something wrong?"

Yeah, your boyfriend was found dead with a bullet in his brain.

"I have a few more questions."

When she stepped aside, I noticed a large diamond dangling from her ear. There was a cinnamon scent in the air that made me think of eggnog. We settled into the same low-slung chairs surrounding her Lucite coffee table.

"I understand your ex-husband was upset over your affair with Elby Salter."

"Isn't that a common reaction?"

"Probably, but what is less uncommon is making threats."

"Fred is impulsive. He lost his cool and blew off some steam. That's all it was."

"I understand that he was stalking Mr. Salter. What do you know about that?"

She let a flip-flop fall off a foot. "Elby told me he thought Fred was following him around, but I told him he was making it up. Elby was just paranoid about the whole thing."

"I have a witness that confirms your ex-husband was stalking him."

"What? You think Fred killed Elby?"

"We're looking at all of Mr. Salter's relationships."

She crossed her legs. "I guess that means me as well?"

"The last time we met, you said that you used the money from the divorce settlement to buy the Mercato house. But that wasn't true, was it? Salter gave you the money to buy it, didn't he?"

Her face reddened. "I wasn't lying. The divorce was taking too long, so Elby lent me the money."

"Oh, something like a bridge loan?"

"Yeah, a bridge loan."

"Did you ever pay off Mr. Salter's loan?"

"Uh, I was going to, but Elby said not to worry about it."

She was getting better at being interviewed, giving an answer that couldn't be verified.

"Did he promise you anything if something happened to him?"

She leaned forward. "Who told you that? Chadwick?"

"Did Mr. Salter make any promises?"

"Elby said a lot of things but nothing like you're trying to say."

"What do you know about Robert Friedman?"

She rolled her eyes. "How he ever got on TV is a mystery to me. You could see his BS a mile away."

"He's a good salesman. He sold Elby on going into business with him."

"Elby hardly ever talked about business. We met Friedman in a restaurant once; that's the only time I met him. He kept calling Elby 'partner' and Elby didn't like it."

"Salter was about as successful as you could get, yet the business he and Friedman had together failed. Do you know why?"

"Like I said, he didn't talk business with me. He'd only say that he had a business dinner to go to on the fifteenth of every month. He could never do anything with me because he had that meeting to go to."

"He never mentioned any problems with Friedman?"

"None that I'm aware of."

"Did you know that Salter was seeing another woman?"

The color drained from her face. Did that suggest she wasn't a gold digger?

"I, I don't know. Are you sure?"

"Her name was Sue."

"How long was this going on?"

"Several weeks before he was murdered."

Her shoulders sagged. "It was probably just a fling . . ."

"Let me ask you, were you having any flings of your own?"

"What kind of a woman do you think I am?"

I was putting together a picture of who she was, but whether the painting would veer to darkness was the question I was going to try my damndest to answer.

**15**

———

I HEADED BACK TO MY OFFICE AFTER GIVING SHERIFF Chester an update on the Salter case. He was as befuddled as I was that the press wasn't playing it up. The sheriff wanted a solve before the family starting applying pressure.

He made it clear we had to step it up and find the killer fast. Chester was up for reelection in two years, and I knew he didn't want a powerful family stirring negatives up.

The pain in my gut resurfaced as I descended the stairs. It was mild but still troubling. Was the pressure Chester heaped on me responsible? Maybe it was nothing but an ulcer. I'd take a boatload of ulcers instead of cancer. I stepped into our office and Derrick said, "Frank, I finally got ahold of Marie Redoux. She was away."

"And she didn't take her phone with her?"

"She was in France visiting family."

"Okay. We need to see her. Let's get going."

"She's working; we'll go there."

Auberge was a traditional French restaurant off Imperial Golf Course Boulevard. As we pulled into the strip center housing the eatery, I wondered if Elby Salter was a member of the exclusive golf course and met her while grabbing a bite for lunch.

There was a lone diner having a late lunch at an outdoor table. Derrick held the door open, and I entered a simply decorated space. Mary Ann and I had been to Paris, and the place reminded me of a bistro we'd eaten in the day we went to Versailles.

I wondered how the moules were here as Derrick asked a busboy to summon Marie. I'd never liked mussels before, but it was on every menu we saw in France, and they ended up being good. Problem was, I needed a loaf of bread to feel full enough.

A bar to my left caught my attention. It was stacked with pastries and colorful piles of macaroons. There was a rack of wine to the right, and I was checking out the labels when I heard footsteps approaching.

Marie Redoux was tall, carrying herself with the confidence I remembered seeing among the people of Paris. She was wearing a country French dress that hugged her curvaceous hips. If she had applied makeup, it wasn't noticeable. Redoux wasn't stunning but was attractive and had a nice smile.

She said something in French to a busboy before greeting me in an accented voice.

"Let's sit over there." Redoux pointed to a corner table by the window. "Can I get you anything? A *café*?"

We declined and sat down on wooden bistro chairs.

I said, "I understand you were in France. How was your trip?"

"Very nice, but the weather was chilly. It's good to be back."

I could listen to her talk all day. Would it get annoying after a while?

"You were born in France?"

"Yes, in Fécamp, on the northern coast by the sea. Maybe you know Le Havre? It's close by."

I decided her voice would never bother me. "Only been there once, mostly the Paris area."

"France is a beautiful country, but the political situation makes me tired. It's not the best place to raise my daughter."

I could see how Elby Salter fell for her smile. "I'm afraid I wouldn't know much about that. Now, I understand you had a relationship with Elby Salter."

She nodded.

"How did you meet him?"

She smiled. "He was on a date, right here, at this very table."

Derrick said, "He was with another woman, and he approached you, in front of her?"

"Elby was discreet. He had questions about the wine list. We only have French wines. I came to the table and gave a recommendation that he accepted. He asked the waiter to have me come by. Elby was going on about the wine, but I knew he was interested in me, and when he went to the toilet, he asked for my number."

After Derrick muttered something about Salter having big balls, he asked, "How long ago was that?"

"One year and a half ago."

I said, "It's our understanding that he broke off the relationship, and that you were unhappy about it."

"No, no. It was time to end it. All things have their time, and ours had passed."

Derrick said, "Why did you call him three times the day before he was killed?"

"Because I had a bottle of the very same wine I recommended the night we first met. I was a little drunk and feeling melancholy."

Her answer came out too quickly; it felt rehearsed. I asked what the wine was, partly to see if she were lying and partly to see if I could find a bottle to try.

"Chêne Bleu, their 2012 Abelard."

I wanted to know where in France it came from but asked, "We've spoken to people who knew about Mr. Salter and you, and they say that you took the breakup hard. That you continually called Mr. Salter and even called his wife."

"Well, that sounds like something his brother would say."

"It wasn't from Chadwick Salter. Now, did you call Elby Salter after the relationship ended?"

"This is getting silly. Was I upset about the harshness Elby showed toward me? Yes. It took a few weeks, but I got over it."

"I understand. Do you know who might have done this to Elby?"

"Well, it wasn't me. I was in France at the time."

An old French saying came to mind: He who excuses himself, accuses himself. Was her trip to France the perfect alibi?

**16**

———————

Fred Baylor didn't want to meet in his office again. I understood, agreeing to meet him at Grouper and Chips. After all, a man has to eat. The strip center that housed the popular eatery was across the street from NCH Downtown.

Baylor was waiting by the front door. We decided to get our lunch and sit at an outdoor table. The place was busy. Most of the tables were occupied by people in scrub outfits. They were here for the food not the decor.

The walls were painted a bright pink to go with a red floor and a neon-lime counter where we placed our order. Mary Ann was nowhere in sight, so I asked for a fried basket of grouper with a side of fries and a Diet Coke. Baylor opted for a blackened grouper platter.

We settled into plastic chairs around the farthest table. As we ate, we talked about the weather (it was hot), baseball (spring training was on), and the rumors a major hotel chain was going to build another tower across from historic Tin City.

Baylor mentioning Tin City was interesting. It was another example of the Salter's influence. The tin-roofed buildings of Tin City had been the hub of commerce and transportation in the 1920s. It was the heart of the Naples fishing industry, with fish-processing plants and boat construction facilities.

As the economic makeup of the area shifted from fishing, the threat was real that Tin City would be replaced by residential units. Wanting to preserve the historic area, the Salters stepped in, retaining it's old Florida charm while transforming it into a mix of shops, dining, and water activities.

IT WAS as good as it gets. I guess that's why fish and chips was so popular in England. I closed my empty clamshell feeling a tinge of guilt. I was going to see the doctor tomorrow, and he wanted me eating healthy. As soon as Baylor finished his lunch, I said, "I have a couple more questions about you and Elby Salter."

He looked at me but said nothing.

"You admitted threatening him. I believe you said it was out of frustration because of the affair your ex-wife was engaged in, but that was it."

"Yeah, that's right."

"How come you didn't tell me that you were stalking Elby Salter?"

"It wasn't stalking. That's crazy."

"Then what was it?"

"I just followed him around a little, that's all. You know, in my car. I'd drive around, make sure he saw me."

"Didn't you also follow him into JetBlue Stadium?"

He exhaled. "That was stupid. I made a mistake. I was pissed off, that's all."

"Are you sure that's all there was?"

"Yeah, of course. I feel like a jerk. I mean, Cindy wasn't even worth it. She was screwing around on him too."

"Your ex-wife was having another affair while seeing Elby?"

"Yep, can you believe it? I'm telling you she was nothing like that when we got married. I don't know what the hell happened to her, but she's not the woman I married."

"If you don't mind me asking, who was the man she was cheating on Elby with?"

"I don't know the last name, but I heard her on the phone one day talking to some guy named Chad."

A piece of fried grouper made its way up my throat. Could it be Chadwick Salter? I needed to process the possibilities, but there was the most important question to ask: "Where were you on the night of February twentieth?"

He stiffened. "You don't think I had anything to do with what happened to that guy, do you?"

"Answer the question, please. Where were you that night?"

"What day of the week was that?"

"A Tuesday."

"I was home that night."

"Are you sure?"

"Yep, no doubt. Mondays I bowl with a bunch of buddies. We're in a league, and well, we tend to overdo the drinking. Tuesdays I keep free to recover. I can't bounce back like I used to."

I knew exactly what he meant by that. My drinking rubber band had been stretched out as well.

"You were home the entire night?"

"Yes."

"Did anyone come by that can vouch for you?"

"No. I was alone, just watching the boob tube."

Why did I want to believe him? Was it because his wife played him for a jerk and I felt for him? He hadn't been honest with me, holding back his harassment of Salter, but was that a sign he was a killer?

------

I HAD Jessie on my lap, and she was sitting upright without much support. "Look at this. Pretty soon she's gonna be walking."

"The way time is flying you're probably right. I still can't believe she's going to be five months old next week."

"It's crazy. You know, if you want to stay home with Jessie, we can swing it for another six months if you want."

"I don't want to keep eating into our savings, Frank. We'll have nothing left if I don't get back to work soon."

"It'd be nice to get a year of paid leave instead of the three months you got. But I guess that would cost way too much."

"We have to decide what's important. I couldn't imagine leaving Jessica after just three months. I'd be a wreck, worrying about her at work."

"I want you home with her for as long as possible. We can do it, and the older she gets the easier it'll be to leave her with someone. Maybe you can ease into it, say three days a week at first."

"I don't know. The way she's growing, I think by the time she's six months old it'll be okay to go back to work."

That was about five weeks away. I hoped it was enough time, not only for Jessie to make the transition, but ample time to resolve whatever was going on in my gut. Having her go back to work with me on the sidelines wouldn't do much for our finances, to say nothing about my mental state.

# 17

DR. BROWN'S WAITING ROOM WAS PACKED. I SIGNED IN AND noticed someone wearing one of those skinny string ties that looked like shoelaces. It was Frank Morgan, who'd served a short stint as sheriff when Joe Liberi had gotten sick.

Morgan was born and raised in Naples and didn't like many of the changes he saw in his hometown. I was a relative newcomer to Southwest Florida when he subbed as sheriff, and he gave me a hard time, viewing me as an outsider. It was weird seeing him here, not only because it was out of context, but also because the murder case I solved when he ran things involved the Boggs, another wealthy family.

Morgan was staring at his cowboy boots when I said, "Sheriff Morgan. How are you?"

"Luca? How are you, son?"

"Good, Sheriff. And you?"

"Getting goddamn old is what I am. What are you doing here?"

Had he forgotten about my bladder cancer? "I come every six months. They have to keep an eye on me."

"Oh geez, sorry, I forgot about your troubles."

"How about you?"

"Damn prostrate acting up. I can't sleep an hour without taking a damn pee."

"Sorry."

"Don't worry about it. You working the Salter homicide?"

"Yeah. Nothing is coming easy though."

"The Salters are an old-line family. Been here longer than mine have."

"I heard they were here from the beginning of the state."

"And I'll tell you, if it weren't for them, this here town and the entire southwest coast wouldn't look like it does. They made sure we didn't turn into another damn Miami."

"How'd they do that?"

"They worked with other developers and landowners to make sure there was a master plan in place. Kept a limit on high-rises and made sure the infrastructure was ahead of the building."

"Well, they sure seem to have made a lot of money doing it."

"Yep, a lot of money, but there was heartbreak."

"It's a shame, he was only fifty-three."

"I ain't talking of Elby. I mean the old man, Prescott, his sister, Florence; she disappeared when I was a teenager."

"Wow. I didn't know that. What happened to her?"

"They never found her. You ask me, it was because the Salters never cooperated with the police."

"Why would they do that?"

"Beats me. They trotted out that privacy thing, but it didn't make any sense to me."

"You think they were involved somehow?"

"I don't really know. After I was on the force a while, I took a look at the case file, but it had nothing."

"It was empty?"

"Nah, just nothing of substance."

The receptionist called Morgan's name, and we said our goodbyes. Waiting the twenty minutes before I was called in was easy as I rolled around what Morgan had said. Was there a connection between Elby's murder and the disappearance and the assumed death of his aunt? What were the odds that two family members met unexplainable departures?

Digging into the Salter family history was something I wanted to do. But what could I learn from previous generations of their clan? It would be interesting but probably a waste of time.

Dr. Brown seemed serious. Did he know something I didn't?

"What's bothering you, Frank?"

"Having a little pain in my belly."

"Show me where."

I touched where it hurt. "Around here. You think it has something to do with my new plumbing?"

"Take your shirt off and lie on the table."

The paper covering the table immediately clung to my back.

"Unbutton the top of your pants."

I knew he was a doctor, but the sound of a male voice making that command was uncomfortable. I dug my chin into my chest and watched him press two fingers into my gut.

"Tell me when you feel something."

I felt a little pull but no real pain. He moved to my lower abdomen.

"Ow. That hurts."

He pressed again. "Here?"

"Yeah."

Hunched over, Dr. Brown silently probed the area. Then he stood up and reached for a pair of gloves.

"Off the table, and drop your drawers, Frank."

"What's going on?"

"Want to check something."

If he told me to put my elbows on the bed, I was running the hell of out of there. I lowered my pants, and he told me to turn my head to the right and cough. He put a gloved hand on my balls. I coughed.

"Cough again."

I complied.

"Turn to the left and cough."

He pawed my balls again, then peeled off the gloves. "You can get dressed now."

I reached for my underwear. "What's going on, Doc? New bladder giving out?"

"No. You have a hernia."

"A hernia?"

"Yes. It looks like you have an incisional hernia. If you remember, I told you that you needed to exercise the abdominal area after surgery to build up the muscle. You haven't done enough, and a hernia developed where the surgeon made an incision."

Even though he criticized my physical condition, I wanted to give him a kiss, now that I was dressed.

"That's a lot better than what I was expecting."

"Hernias are common, but yours was avoidable if you would have followed post-operative instructions."

I let the lecture go, after all, it was a hernia, not cancer. "What's the next step?"

"Surgery to repair the rip. It usually is done with a laparoscope. It's not too invasive."

"How long until I am back on my feet?"

"A couple of days, maximum. You'll be sore the first two or three days, but you'll be able to get around."

"I'm working a case now; can I wait to get this done?"

"I wouldn't ignore it; these tears can expand, and then you'll have a much larger problem."

He didn't trust me because I'd missed a few days at the gym? "I'm not going to ignore it. Just wanted to know if I could postpone the surgery for a couple of weeks or so."

"There's a risk with delaying any necessary procedure, but if you feel you must, I wouldn't let it go past six weeks."

He gave me the name of a surgeon but told me to check with the team of doctors who removed my bladder and made my new plumbing.

I left the office feeling good. It wasn't anything major, and I'd be around to watch Jessie grow up.

**18**

---

Staring at the Salter whiteboard, my lower back started to ache. It wasn't giving me anything. I said to Derrick, "One of the most useful things you can do in a homicide investigation, and it's simple, is to take stock of where you are, what you have, especially in cases where there are multiple threads, no real primary path to pursue."

"I remember you telling me that the first week I got here. We going to do that with Salter?"

"Yep." I tapped Elby Salter's photo. "A fifty-three-year-old man, from one of the oldest and wealthiest families in the county, is killed mob style. Married, no children. He carried on affairs, sometimes two at a time. Was charitable. Liked baseball and owned interests in too many businesses to count. Had a shady partner. That's probably not fair to Friedman; let's call him oily. He needs a closer look."

"I'll dig into him."

"Good. Now, there could be a connection to his murder with his screwing around. Something driven by passion or financial gain."

"Cindy Baylor. She got the money from Salter to buy the Mercato house. That's a million dollars' worth of motive."

"But Salter didn't seem to want the money back. Maybe he viewed it as the price of admission."

"Yeah, but he had this new woman. Maybe he was dumping Baylor and wanted his money back."

"These people are worth billions. I can't see him getting into it with her over the house money. It has to be more than that, much more. Nobody in this case is the type to kill over money unless its megadough. A big insurance payoff, or crazy as it sounds, access to a bank account or something for her if he died."

"I can't see how she could get any money out of him being dead. She needed him around to bankroll her lifestyle."

"You're right. But there's the slimmest chance he set something up to take care of her."

"You think so?"

"I doubt it, but we have to keep our eyes open about it."

"What about her husband?"

"You know, before he told me about her cheating on Elby, he was near the top of the list with the stalking thing. But now I don't think he did anything more than any wounded man would."

"Not me. My wife screws around on me, it's over. I'd erase her from my life in a second."

Derrick was too young to understand how people find themselves turned upside down. "It's not as easy as you think. I agree with you, but it's a lot more complicated than that."

"What's so complicated about a wife cheating?"

"I'm not saying it's acceptable and that you should forgive her, but you have to look at the whole picture. That's all I'm saying. Let's not get sidetracked here. We need to poke around and see if we can find any evidence Fred Baylor was seen outside his home that night."

"We should canvass his neighborhood. See what we can dredge up."

"Farm it out to the foot soldiers. Go see McQuire. Tell him what we need."

"Now?"

"No. We're not done going through all this. There is something about this family. I ran into Sheriff Morgan, he's an old-timer, was born here. He told me something about the Salter family. Years ago, a sister of Elby's father went missing and never turned up."

"Really? You think it's related?"

"It'd be crazy if it was, and I can't see how. But there is something with this family. They seem to be nice enough people, but I can't put it into words . . ."

"They're rich as all hell. I told Lynn a bit about the case after we found out who he was, and she said she knew them from when she was up in Orlando. They own a ton of property up there, thousands of acres of sugarcane farms and a bunch of developments. You know, she said that they even donated the land that the Kennedy Space Center is built on."

"Are you kidding me? The Space Center?"

The phone rang and Derrick answered it. He stood up, shaking his head and hung up.

"We got another corpse."

"Where?"

"Naples Dock. Some guy was going to take his family out for a ride, and when he went below, there was a body."

THE MAIN DOCK was cordoned off with yellow tape. A crowd of boaters and tourists were milling around. We snuck under the tape, signed in, and headed toward a group of officers fifty yards away. The smell of diesel fuel permeated the air.

It was the first time I'd been back here since the Serenity case. There was the thinnest of threads connecting the cases —wealthy people and boats. But that was how my mind worked. I discounted it as we got to the stern of the boat where the body was.

It was a twenty-five-foot Viking with a small cabin. A nice boat, but nothing remotely like the ones the people on Keewaydin owned. A balding man in shorts and Top-Siders was talking to the officers. We needed to see the scene before talking to anyone.

We pulled on gloves. Derrick jumped on board and offered his hand. I declined. Tugging the tie-up line to bring the boat closer, the pain in my gut erupted. Did he think I was getting too old to jump like he did? Or was he considering the hernia I had?

I pulled the latch on the teak door leading below. A pair of feet in black shoes were visible. The stainless stairs were steeper than K2. Descending, I held both rails. The shoes were connected to legs in black slacks. I took another step. The waist area was visible. The corpse's hands were bound.

A pool of blood around the victim's head had a darker tinge to it. It was no longer spreading. It appeared to be a shot to the base of the skull, just like Salter. I put my other foot on the ground, stepping toward the body. Was this another execution of a rich man?

Derrick scrambled down the stairs into the tiny space. "Holy shit. It's exactly like Salter."

Crouching by the head I said, "Not quite. This poor bastard had a rag stuffed down his throat."

Derrick circled around me. "He almost looks like the guy in the sketch, doesn't he?"

He was right. The dead man looked similar to the man the artist had drawn of the guy at the scene of Elby Salter's murder. Could it be the same man? If so, who the hell was he?

**19**

———



Mary Ann said, "I'm going to give her a quick bath."

"Now? She's already cranky."

"Everyone was holding her today. And some of the baptismal oil dripped down her neck. Thank God it didn't get on her dress."

"She looked amazing in her christening gown."

"It's on the bed. Hang it up, please. I want to get it preserved."

Did she have plans for a second kid? "For what?"

"So she'll have it when she's older. Maybe one of her kids will wear it."

Jessica is not even a half year old, and Mary Ann's talking about her having a baby?

I hung up the lace gown and admired it. It was beautiful: white satin with embroidered lace embellishments. The price of it and its length initially annoyed me, but I couldn't imagine Jessie in anything else.

Changing into shorts and a T-shirt, I heard Mary Ann kissing Jessie. She came into the bedroom. Jessica was bundled in a towel. She smelled wonderful. I sneaked a kiss in as Mary Ann dressed her in pajamas covered with the alphabet. Jessie's eyes were slits. Mary Ann put her down, and seconds later she was sleeping.

Mary Ann collapsed into a chair in the family room, and I spread out on the couch.

"She's an angel, Frank."

"I know. She didn't even cry like the other kids when the priest anointed her. The kid's got a great disposition. Takes after her father."

"Yeah, right. Mr. Moody."

"It's called having a diverse personality."

"You're impossible."

"What about Derrick? He's great with Jessie, isn't he?"

"He's a good guy. And I really like Lynn. She wants to be a mom. I'll bet they have a kid right away."

"When are they getting married?"

"Next year. I think in April."

"That's nice."

"You don't have any excuse now that Jessica is christened."

"Excuse for what?"

"To get your hernia fixed."

Ugh.

---

I WAS LATE GETTING to work and stepped into the office slowly.

Derrick said, "You okay?"

"Yeah."

"You're walking like you got a pole up your ass."

"Frigging surgeon was rough giving me an exam."

"Some doctors are like that, aren't they?"

"Why? I'll never know."

"What did he say?"

"It's a she. I'm scheduled get the hernia repaired in two weeks."

"I don't know if I could have a woman doctor poking around down there."

I lowered myself into a chair. "After what I went through with the bladder cancer, nothing could embarrass me."

"You're right. Look, I have that witness who helped with the composite drawing coming in to take a look at the body found on the boat."

"Good. But we're still going to need an ID."

"I know. Hey, I made a couple of calls this morning on Friedman, and it looks like he may be in some financial trouble."

"Interesting. How someone could blow through all the money he must have made with those infomercials is beyond me."

"That's if he made any money at all. I heard at least half of those products never even sell enough to cover the production."

"Maybe if they put them on at a reasonable hour, they'd have a chance to break even."

Derrick grabbed his jacket. "I'm out of here. You going to lie low?"

"No. I'm going to see Chadwick."

---

ELBY'S BROTHER'S house wasn't as large or as well kept. However, it did have a porch that seemed to encircle the house. A long, rectangular pool was populated with four arching streams of water, reminding me of submerged loops. I never liked fountains, but it was nice.

Parking next to a blue Mustang, I noticed someone sitting on the front porch. It was Chadwick. It appeared I not only wouldn't get inside the house, I wouldn't even get to stare at the Gulf as we talked.

The gravel crunching under my feet mixed with the sound of the fountain. I eyed the stairs; there were just three. I'd suck up the discomfort. The handrail was rough. Before I hit the second step, Chadwick came over.

We shook hands and he said, "Let's sit over here."

I followed him to a pair of settees with flowered cushions. On top of the glass-topped wicker table that separated the seating was a bowl of fruit, a plate of assorted sandwiches, a pitcher of lemonade, and one with water. It was only 11 a.m. Had Chadwick put thought into my visit, or did the Salters live better than I had imagined?

I sank onto a sofa, the sound of the water putting me in a mini trance. "This is a nice place you have here."

"Been in the family for years. My granddaddy used to live here."

"And having your brother right next door must have been nice."

"It was."

The way he said it meant it wasn't.

He covered it with, "By the way, if you're hungry, feel free."

"Thanks."

"What can I do for you, Detective?"

I leaned forward. "Are you having an affair with Cindy Baylor?"

Chadwick swiveled his head toward the window behind him. It was closed. He lowered his voice. "Detective Luca, this is my home. Your question is not only inappropriate, it has no relevancy to my brother's murder."

I whispered, "You lied to me. Why?"

At low volume, you could feel the sound waves in his deep-bass voice. "I beg to differ. I believe I've been truthful; however, I don't see the purpose of discussing private matters."

"You're having an affair with the same woman as your murdered brother."

He stuck a fork into the fruit plate, plucking out a melon ball. He ate it and put the utensil down.

"Are you going to admit to this?"

"Unless you have proof that it is related to my brother's passing, I am not going to address what is a private matter."

"Fair enough."

Reaching for my lemonade, I tried to make sense of the situation. I couldn't see a grown sibling killing a brother over an affair. Screwing around with another man's spouse was a different story. I imagined there was an abundant supply of women for the Salter brothers to engage with. Why Cindy Baylor? She was no slouch, but she wasn't Marilyn Monroe either. Was it the maddening need for privacy that led them to share a girlfriend?

"Let me ask you a related question. Did Fred Baylor ever come after you or stalk you when he found out about you and Cindy?"

"He did for a while. I didn't notice him at first, but Cindy spotted him once, and I knew I had to be careful."

"Did he ever threaten you?"

"Not directly, but knowing he was out there was uncomfortable, to say the least."

So, he was uncomfortable because he was being watched

and not because he was cheating on his wife with another man's wife?

"Let me ask you about your brother's interests."

"You mean besides the Red Sox?"

"He was a big fan, wasn't he?"

"He tried to get them to move into Collier."

"I thought they were building a new stadium here."

"I don't think it will ever happen."

"Why is that?"

"Just a feeling, that's all."

"In regard to Elby's business interests, I know we talked about Robert Friedman before, but is there anyone else he had dealings with that you believe was of suspect character?"

"I'm sure there were. I didn't get involved in his deals, but Friedman is a leech."

He couldn't provide anything concrete except color. I left Chadwick knowing I needed to take a closer look at Friedman. But the real takeaway was trying to figure out who was lying: Fred Baylor or Chadwick? And why?

**20**

———

Now that I was a father, my sympathy for parents with sick children had deepened. I couldn't imagine what happens to those who lose a child. How could they overcome the loss? It was more like finding a way to live with the grief rather than putting it behind you.

Elby Salter's father had taken his son's death hard, we were told. I understood completely and had given him time before speaking with him.

I turned off Crayton Road onto Mermaids Bight, a curvy street that backed up to Doctors Bay. Thinking how cool it was to say you lived on a street with such a great name, I caught a glimpse of water between the monstrous houses lining the street.

Near the end of the road was the only single-story structure on the block. It was where Prescott Salter lived. I pulled into the driveway, and the front door opened. Was it a maid or a nurse?

"You must be Detective Luca. I'm Emma. I look after Mr. Salter."

"Nice to meet you, Emma."

"Follow me. Mr. S is out back."

She led me on a paver path alongside the home. Wondering what was in the Salter DNA that made the insides of their homes taboo, I squinted. The bay sparkled. It wasn't the biggest house on the block, but I couldn't imagine one with longer views.

A boat was making its way under Harbor Drive to my left. To the left lay Venetian Village. The rooftop bar at Bayside was empty. I was wondering if you could hear their music from here when I heard a slider open.

A walker hit the deck ahead of Prescott Salter. Emma stood close by but didn't offer assistance.

He straightened his thin frame and extended a hand covered with liver spots.

"Prescott Salter, young man. You're a detective, aren't you?"

"Yes, sir. Homicide. My name's Frank Luca."

"Take any seat anywhere you like, Mr. Luca, except this one."

Emma pulled a chair into the direct sun, and Prescott Salter eased into it.

"Thank you, Emma. I suspect Mr. Luca would like to speak privately." He winked at me.

The aide stepped toward the door. "I'll leave you boys out here. Let me know if you need me, Mr. S."

Prescott fumbled with the buttons of his sweater as a soft breeze blew through.

"You're here about my son, aren't you?"

"Yes, and I'd like to offer my condolences for your loss, sir."

"Accepted. Now, why don't you get to what you wanted."

"In an investigation, we like to speak with those who

knew the victim best. I would have come sooner, but I realize how difficult this is for you and wanted to give you as much time as possible."

"Life is filled with difficulty. You get to my age, just going to the bathroom is challenging."

He should only know my story. "You seem to be doing pretty good."

There was a light knock and a slider opened. Emma was carrying a tray with a pitcher of iced tea. She set it on the table and poured glasses for us. She looked at me. "It's unsweetened. There's sugar in the bowl."

She disappeared into the house, and Prescott grabbed the bowl and scooped a spoonful into his glass.

"Now, get to it, Detective, before she tries to get me to take a nap."

I took a sip and set the glass down. "You seem like a man who likes to get to the point."

"Indeed, I am. I never quite understood all the circuitous chatter folks engage in to get to what they really wanted to say."

Being a detective would be frustrating for him. "Who do you think could have murdered your son?"

He brushed at a drop of condensation that had fallen from his glass onto his sweater. "I'm eighty-three years old, Detective. How would I know?"

"I was hoping you'd have some insights about his business interests."

"My son was a grown man. He made his own decisions."

"Did you agree with those decisions?"

His hazel eyes flashed. "You seem like you have some intelligence, Detective. You should know that no two people can agree on everything."

Some intelligence? "Mr. Salter, I'm sure a man of your intellect would understand the meaning of my question."

"Touché, Detective."

"Were there particular business decisions you disagreed with?"

"The Salter family has extensive holdings throughout the Southeast and in Florida, where we've been since the formation of this great state. My sons, like the sons of my forefathers, make mistakes. It's as simple as that. He's a grown man, and like all of us, must live with the consequences."

That seemed at odds with the man and the family that had set up a trust with rules. But he was an old man dealing with the loss of his son. Maybe it was his way of dealing with the pain.

"I understand you lost a sister years ago."

He blinked twice. "Is the purpose of your visit to tarnish the Salter name?"

"Absolutely not, sir. I'm a homicide detective investigating your son's murder. I wouldn't be doing my job if I didn't explore every connection to a case."

"Florence disappeared over forty years ago. So much for your connection, Detective."

Emma came out of the house. "Excuse me, Mr. S, it's pill time."

She gave him a handful of medicines and watched him down them before going back inside.

"Don't get old, son."

"Is there anything you think we should look into? A person or business interest that might have something to do with your son's murder?"

"I've given this more thought than anything else in my life. It was senseless. Elby was a good son, not perfect, but who the hell is?"

"I appreciate your time, Mr. Salter. We'll solve this homicide."

He held out a hand. "Preferably, quickly and quietly."

**21**

———

Mary Ann came out of the bedroom, her hair and Jessica wrapped in towels. On the couch, I said, "Bring the peanut over."

Mary Ann placed Jessie in my arms. I inhaled deeply. The smell of a clean baby was life-affirming. Jessie's eyes were heavy.

"Say good night to Daddy."

I kissed my daughter and handed her off to Mary Ann, who said, "What are you watching?"

"Oh, this is good. It's a documentary about a secret group called the Bilderberg. You know me, I don't buy conspiracy theories, but this group has been going since the early fifties."

"What do they do?"

"According to this, they're deep into public policy around the world. They make decisions that impact everyone."

"How come we never heard about them?"

"They're crazy about secrecy."

"What about your saying that the only way to keep a secret between two people is when one of them is dead."

"Very funny, Mary Ann. Watch it; you'll see what I mean.

These guys have armed guards at their meetings and planes flying overhead to keep it secure. They don't want any press coverage."

"Aw, come on, Frank. You believe that?"

"It's real. There's all kinds of powerful people in it."

"Like who?"

"A lot of businessmen and powerful families. Even government figures like Ben Bernanke, the guy who was the head of the Federal Reserve. He was a member."

"Really? What do they do at these meetings?"

"Nobody knows for sure, but they're saying that they get together to discuss what they want done across the world, things like a common government or using the same money. Kind of like what they're trying to do in Europe."

"How could they do that?"

"These are powerful people, Mary Ann. If a guy like Bernanke decides to do something with America's monetary policy, it'll get done, and the world will follow. Believe me. And say, if all the business people agree to invest in turning seawater into something drinkable or building more or less parks, it happens."

An image of old man Salter popped into my head—what Sheriff Morgan had said about the Salters working to make this place what it was.

"I have to get her to bed."

"Good night, Jessie."

I turned back to the TV. That groups like this existed fascinated me.

---

THERE WAS a cup of coffee on my desk but no Derrick in the office. I picked up the cup, and it was warm. Sipping the java,

I scrolled through my in-box, looking for something from forensics and wondering if the Salters were part of a secret organization.

Nothing. We still hadn't gotten an ID on the body from the marina. It was looking more like the corpse was an illegal immigrant. Who was this guy? The only clue we had was a tattoo with the word *Libertad*: the Spanish word for freedom. Not much help on who he was, or why he was killed.

The only lead on the killing, if you could call it that, was a sighting that a boat had come into the marina late the night before the body was discovered. It only had its running lights on and had been seen leaving the dock area where the body was found. That was all we had. Next to nothing.

Derrick swung into the office waving a handful of papers.

"Friedman is up to his eyeballs in debt. His house is in foreclosure."

"Interesting."

"Interesting? You want to know what's interesting?"

"Get to it, Derrick."

"He filed a suit against none other than Elby Salter."

"What? When was this?"

"Two weeks before he was murdered."

"What was the basis for it?"

"This is a summary I got from the court filing. He claimed that Salter reneged on promises he made to pay Friedman an exit fee if they terminated the partnership."

"Was it in a contract or something?"

"Nope. All verbal, according to Friedman."

"Sounds like he was a mosquito looking to suck blood, betting that Salter would pay to make him go away."

"And it didn't work, so he killed him."

"I don't know if he leapt from a lawsuit to a killing, but it's a line we need to pursue. Something would have to have happened to motivate Friedman from trying to squeeze money out of him to murdering him."

"He needed money. What other reason do you need?"

He was right. I'd put a fair share of greedy killers behind bars. "Amen. We need to grill Friedman. Why didn't he tell us he had sued Salter?"

"Because he knew how it would look."

"I don't know. So, he sues Salter, and we're assuming it didn't go his way. Friedman doesn't get anything, or what he views as not enough, and is so pissed he hires someone to kill Salter. It's happened before. Someone goes through the system to right what they believe is a wrong, and when the outcome is not what they expect, they take the law into their own hands."

"It's more than plausible. Plus, Friedman is a slickster."

"He'd have to be desperate to go from huckster to killer. That's a huge jump. We need to dig as deep as we can; see if there is evidence of violence in his past. If there is something there, then this becomes a possible scenario."

"I'm on it, Frank. I'll see what's there."

"We still need to find out about Elby's new girlfriend, Sue."

"You have any ideas on how to track her down?"

"I never met a woman who didn't know who her rival was."

"Amen. Lynn still brings up Valeria every now and then."

"I think we start by asking Elby's wife and Cindy Baylor and the French gal about her."

"Maybe Weaver knows some others he dated."

## 22

DERRICK WAS READING THE NEWSPAPER WHEN I CAME IN. HE stuck it in a drawer.

"Morning, Frank."

"Morning. You read the paper to get depressed?"

"I like to keep up with the local happenings. Hey, did you know the deal for the new Red Sox stadium was squashed?"

I took a sip of coffee. "No. What happened?"

"Something about the developers and the contract for the land."

"When did this happen?"

"The article said yesterday."

"You know, when I went to see Chadwick Salter, he said it wasn't going to happen. But that was over a week ago. How could he have known about it?"

"They got connections, you know that."

I certainly did. "I want you to dig around; find out who was behind killing the deal. Who was involved, how they ended what looked like a done deal, and why. I'm betting the Salters are involved."

"Could be, but if they are, what's the significance?"

"If I knew, we'd be chasing that down already. Let's see what you find out."

It was possible the stadium thing could be related. Elby was a huge Red Sox fan. He wanted the team and the players he loved closer. He'd also raise his profile with the team, engineering a deal for a new stadium packed with amenities.

Did he step on someone's toes? Powerful business interests opposed to moving the team out of Fort Myers would resist. It could be one of them. Then there were the people against having the team in Collier.

Was the deal opposed by Elby's own family because of their interests, and with Elby dead, they killed the deal? There were hundreds of millions of dollars at stake. At the end of the day, sports was big business. Sports and team loyalty occupied an unhealthy obsession in a good slug of the population. Could moving a team prompt an unstable fan to murder? It would seem far-fetched to most people, but not to a homicide detective.

DERRICK CAME into the office shaking his head.

"No dice. Guy couldn't identify the marina body as the man he saw the night Salter was killed."

"Damn it. I was hoping we'd get a bead on him. How the hell we going to solve it if we don't even know who he is?"

"Don't have a clue."

"If it's not connected to the Salter case, then we table it. Sooner or later someone is going to come looking for this guy. Tell Sally to put a statewide alert that matches what we've got on the body. Maybe someone filed a missing person that matches our corpse."

QUAIL CREEK'S dining room was bustling and louder than I remembered. I walked to the same table Friedman had been at the last time, nearly needing to put my sunglasses on. Wearing a yellow sports jacket, Friedman looked like a canary. His porcelain veneers flashed an LED white as he chatted with a waitress.

He put down a glass of brown liquid with a cherry when he saw me.

"How are we doing today?"

"All is good, Mr. Friedman."

"Sit down. You want something?"

"No thanks."

"What's going on with the Elby case?"

"I have a couple of questions for you."

He sipped his drink. "Shoot."

"How come you never told me you filed a lawsuit against Elby Salter?"

"What's the big deal? Let me tell you, he was the defendant in many proceedings."

I'd have to circle back. "Let's stick to the one you filed."

"Am I missing something, Detective? We were in business, and I sued him. Unfortunately, it's not an unusual development between partners."

"You filed the suit two weeks before he was murdered."

"How could I know that someone would kill him? It didn't exactly help my case, with him out of the picture."

"Were you trying to extort money out of him?"

"Extort? That's crazy. I filed a lawsuit to settle our differences."

"My sources tell me it was a frivolous filing aimed at getting Salter to settle it."

Friedman's eyes narrowed. "Frivolous? You have any idea of the promises he made to me?"

"I understand you claim those assurances were made verbally."

"That doesn't make them any less valid. Courts consider oral contracts all the time."

"You needed the money, didn't you?"

"Of course, I did. I'm sixty-five. Why else would I get involved with a court case unless I had to."

He was sixty-seven, but I let it slide; the fib fit his physical doctoring. "I understand you are in some financial trouble."

"Life has its ups and downs. Right now, I'm riding low, but I'll bounce back. I always do."

"Your home is in foreclosure."

"It's a house, that's all. I don't worry about material things at this stage of my life."

I wanted to ask him if he ever heard of saving some of the money he made. "Did you try to settle your disagreement before going to court?"

"Of course, I did. He wouldn't hear of it. We were friends, not close, but nonetheless friends. He'd give me the business-is-business line, saying he had to keep things separate."

"That must have made you angry."

"Of course, it did."

"Mad enough to seek revenge?"

"Look, I took my grievances to a lawyer and we sued. That's all I did."

Friedman wasn't the type to have shot Salter himself, but could he have hired someone to do it?

"You've been in business with a couple of colorful people in your career."

He sighed. "You're going to bring up the fulfillment business? That was twenty years ago."

"You were partners with the Salido brothers, one of whom is serving life for manslaughter."

"Oh, come on, now. I needed warehousing and pick-and-pack services in New Jersey. It's all union; you couldn't do anything without them."

"Did you ask the Salidos to settle a score for you?"

His shoulders sagged. "No, that's crazy. I'm an old man; how much time you think I have left?"

Time passed quickly, but Friedman had stepped on the accelerator. "Tell me about some of the other lawsuits that were filed against Elby Salter."

His vigor returned. "I don't know much detail, but Elby, he had a habit of promising people things, like he did with me. It pissed people off." He paused before saying, "I heard he used it with the women as well."

"Do you have any specifics?"

**23**

---

Derrick breezed into the office as I was hanging up the phone.

"I guess it's no surprise Chadwick is the executor of his brother's estate."

"Could have been the old man."

"Nah, people like the Salters are master planners. Prescott probably was at some point, but he passed it on. It makes sense."

"What did Chadwick say?"

"Bottom line, all of Elby's assets either went or are heading into the Salter family trust. Annabelle is getting something, but he wouldn't elaborate. They had a prenup, and Elby had a will."

"Can't she contest it? They were married like twenty years. That's a long time."

"She could, but it'd be a waste of time and money on lawyers."

"What about the Friedman lawsuit? He say anything about that?"

"Not specifically, but he said something interesting when

I mentioned it. He said any pending legal proceedings would either be dismissed or settled if there was a legal basis to do so."

"Pending? How many lawsuits could they be involved in?"

"Exactly what I was thinking. Now, we have to remember that these people are involved in a lot of deals, and there are bound to be disagreements. How deep and emotional those differences are is what I'm interested in exploring."

"Should we do a search?"

I didn't want to tell him we should have done it already. "Yes, I want to see what is out there, both civilly and criminally."

**24**

———————

I CROSSED MY ARMS OVER MY CHEST AND MOVED TO THE corner of the room. The flimsy gown was no match for the air-conditioning. I kept telling myself it was a minor procedure, but considering my bout with cancer, an upset stomach was cause for concern. If I were in charge, I'd make sure you'd get a Valium before you did the paperwork.

It was difficult to distract myself as I waited. Concentrating on Jessica lasted only a couple of minutes. Shifting, I thought about the Salter case. The fact that Elby Salter had been behind the stadium land deal had to be an important clue. It was something he was passionate about, and it was reversed within weeks of his death.

Powerful forces were aligned against the deal, including his own family. How far would they go to prevent it from happening? There was no shortage of resources at their disposal, but did their stockpile include an assassin?

The line Michael Corleone said to Kate in *The Godfather* concerning her naiveté over politicians ordering killings came to mind as a nurse poked her head in.

"Come with me, Mr. Luca. They're ready for you now."

They might be ready, but I wasn't. I trudged behind her into a brightly lit room and hopped onto a gurney. They hooked an IV in me, and the last thing I remember was an image of Michael Corleone standing beside a 1950s black Cadillac.

---

"MARY ANN! MARY ANN!"

She came into the bedroom holding Jessie. "What's the matter?"

"I can't get out of bed."

"What?"

"Every time I move, I get this stabbing feeling like someone's jabbing a knife in my gut."

"It's completely normal. Don't you remember what the doctor said?"

I shrugged. "Just help me swing my legs off the bed."

"You have to move around. They told you that, Frank."

"But it hurts like hell."

"You'll be okay. It'll pass. Don't worry. Isn't that what you said when I was in labor?"

"Ha-ha. You know what? Don't help me. I'll get up myself."

Mary Ann shook her head and left the bedroom.

What, did she forget that I had all new plumbing put in me? Maybe that was the reason it was hurting so much. I ask for a little help, and she gets like a North Korean drill instructor?

I inched my legs to the edge of the bed. Putting a hand on the nightstand, I rose as slowly as a weed. The pinching was painful, but I kept my mouth shut. Standing felt better. I shuffled to the bathroom with minimal pain, dreading that I'd have to sit to pee.

Fortunately, going to the bathroom wasn't as bad as I'd feared. I washed up and headed to the kitchen.

"Here comes Daddy, Jessica."

I wanted to hold her, but the doctor said lifting was out. I gave her a kiss and ambled to the coffeemaker.

"You feeling okay?"

"Yep."

"See, all you have to do is move around a little, and in a couple of days you'll be back to normal."

Rather than say anything, I nodded, put a pod in the machine and banked her statement about moving around a little for future use.

———

BEING home and not feeling great was no picnic. I'd rather be working. At least time would fly, and I'd do something useful with the day. Messing around with Jessie was fun, but I'd get bored after half an hour. I wasn't supposed to drive or leave the house.

The lanai was the perfect place for a nap. I lowered myself onto a chaise and hoped I'd grab an hour of sleep. I tried to quiet my thoughts, but that only seemed to work when I was dead tired. Before the pulsing in my gut ended, I was back thinking of the Salter case.

There was a lot of work to be done. Derrick was out interviewing, and here I was on my back. Regretting that I had my hernia repaired, I got up slowly and went into the den. Connecting to my office desktop, I pulled down a telephone number and dialed.

"Fred Baylor? This is Detective Luca."

"Uh, yes. How are you doing?"

He didn't need to know. "Good. I wanted to ask you a question."

"This is really not a good time. I've got a meeting to attend."

"I'm sorry. It will only take a moment."

"Okay, go ahead."

"Did you follow Chadwick Salter?"

"Look, I told you about trailing Elby. It was stupid, but that was it."

"So, you didn't stalk Chadwick Salter?"

A pause long enough to tie a sneaker. "No, I didn't"

"Are you sure you don't want to reconsider that response?"

"I never stalked him."

"That's funny, because he said you did and that your ex-wife, Cindy, knew about it."

"It wasn't anything like stalking."

Ah, the all-important qualifier. "Then what was it?"

"I followed them twice; that was it. Then I realized what a jerk I was being. She wasn't the woman I married. I had to be crazy to give a shit about her. Making a mistake once, maybe, but there she was with someone else."

"I want to believe you, Fred, I really do, but why didn't you come clean the first time?"

"You know how embarrassing this is?"

"Why didn't you tell me?"

"I wanted to, I swear. I was afraid, that's all."

Swearing had lost its cachet. "With all the lying you did, I should arrest you for obstruction."

"No, please. I swear, I had nothing to do with what happened to Elby Salter."

"If I find out you've been lying again, I'm coming after you hard."

The fact he stalked Chadwick, as well took him down a notch on the suspect ladder, Baylor was one of those guys who thought he could lie to the police and get away with it. The reality was it discounted every other word they uttered.

**25**

---

I TOLD DERRICK ABOUT THE ANONYMOUS CALL THAT HAD just come in.

"Why did this guy call it in, Frank?"

"I don't know. Maybe they get to keep some of the money if they don't have to pay a claim."

"That's probably it."

"I don't care. I'm glad he did."

"She's going to get ten million?"

"Yeah, the face value of the life insurance was five million, and murder qualifies as an accidental death. They had coverage for it, and the benefit doubled."

"That sounds like strong motivation, but five mil is not a lot for people like them."

"No doubt, but don't forget the kind of marriage they had. This guy was out there banging anything he could. Annabelle knew it, couldn't do anything about it. Maybe she felt trapped."

"Yeah, if she divorced him, I'm sure she'd lose whatever they were giving her."

"Who was paying the premium on it? It had to be expensive."

"Was it a second-to-die policy? A lot of married people have that kind."

I was married now and didn't have any life insurance. I was afraid my cancer history would make it prohibitive, but if something happened to me or the both of us, Jessie would need money. It was something I had to tend to.

"No, it was just on her. Maybe the trust had enough life insurance on him."

"It makes sense to have life insurance when you're married. Is that when she got covered?"

"No, the policy was written six years ago."

"What precipitated that?"

"It's one of the questions I have."

IT WAS another place I'd never heard of, the Naples Depot Museum. The old train depot was dressed Mediterranean style, despite its mission to educate the goings-on of the Roaring Twenties.

Poking my head inside, I saw Annabelle. She was talking to another volunteer in front of a restored mule wagon. The wooden vehicle looked new. I headed in a little too quickly and felt a twinge in my gut. A small group of kids was gathered in front of an interactive exhibit. Their excitement made me want to bring Jessie here.

Annabelle waved.

"This is a cool place. I never knew it existed."

"I know. Most people don't know anything about all the museums we have in Collier. It's a great place to volunteer."

"The kids seem to like it."

"We have a beautifully restored train car out back. You get a good picture of how Naples evolved from a sleepy village in the 1880s to what it is today."

"When my daughter is a little older, we'll take her over."

"Let me know. I'll give her the VIP treatment."

She was a different person than the one I met at her oceanfront house. "Thanks. Why don't we talk outside?"

"Thank you for meeting me here. With all the boxes, the house is upside down."

"You're moving?"

"Yes. The home is in the trust's name."

"Who is moving in?"

"I don't really know. But Chad always loved the house."

"But he's right next door."

"Yes, but this is the Salter crown jewel. Chad's place is, well, let's just say it's not as prominent."

"Is Chadwick the jealous type?"

"Competitive would be a better way to describe him."

Interesting. "I see. Was Chadwick opposed to Elby's involvement in trying to move the Red Sox into Collier?"

"In the beginning, Elby made some comment he was giving him a hard time, but it was nothing like the other crazies who came out of the woodwork."

"What do you mean by that?"

"Elby received two or three letters in the mail making threats about moving the team."

"Do you have the letters?"

"No. Elby discarded them. He didn't take them seriously."

"Did you?"

"Not really. He showed me one, and it appeared that a child had written it. He said the team received all kinds of letters from fans mad about this or that."

"People do take their sports seriously."

"Very true, and at the expense of the arts."

"I wanted to ask you about the life insurance policy on your husband."

There was no tell. "What about it?"

"It seems unusual for the Salter family to have insurance outside of the trust."

"What is so unusual about having a wife being the beneficiary of a policy on her husband?"

It was a good question, but I had the badge. "I understand, with the accident provision, you're going to collect ten million dollars."

"Yes, that's correct."

"When did you get the policy?"

"About seven years ago."

"And you were married about twenty-three years, correct?"

"Twenty-four."

"Why would you wait seventeen years to get life insurance? It had to be cheaper when he was younger."

"It's no secret we didn't have the best of marriages. Time was passing, and I felt exposed, especially without children. Without anyone to carry on the"—she fingered quotes—"Salter name, the family discounted me."

"But I understand there are provisions in the trust to take care of you if something were to happen to Elby."

"Look, I wasted years of my life. That's not fair. In the beginning things were good. But when it became apparent I was unable to bear his children, things started to fall apart."

"And you pressed him to provide security?"

"You could say that. I'd phrase it as earning it though."

"Why didn't you simply divorce him?"

"I wish I could answer that."

"Did you have anything to do with your husband's death?"

"Absolutely not."

"What do you believe happened to him?"

"Elby had traits that were bound to get him in trouble."

"You mean his various affairs?"

She started to say no, then hesitated. "That was part of it."

"What were you about to say?"

"Nothing. There's nothing more I have to say."

"Come on, Mrs. Salter. We're investigating your husband's murder. Every shred of information is important."

"Elby was a good man, but he had his faults like the rest of us."

"Was it drugs or alcohol?"

"No."

"Gambling?"

"No, Elby had too much respect for money."

"Pornography?"

She shook her head. "No."

She was hiding something. What was it?

"What do you know about the disappearance of Elby's aunt, Florence?"

"Not much. The family hardly ever spoke about her."

"What was the speculation on what had happened to her?"

"I don't know, but Prescott insinuated that she was not mentally stable and had gotten in trouble."

"Any idea on the type of trouble?"

"None."

"Okay. Are you sure you don't have anything to add about Elby?"

She averted her eyes and shook her head.

She was concealing something, but whether it would help the case or was a personal matter was the question.

## 26

———

Derrick and I jumped into the Cherokee. Before I had a chance to process the interview with Annabelle, a gaping hole in Fred Baylor's story opened up.

"How's the hernia feeling?"

"I can hardly feel it. I know it's there, but it's not really bothering me anymore."

"Great. So, tell me what Salter's wife said."

"There's something there. Annabelle was hiding something."

"What did she say?"

"It's what she didn't say. That and her body language."

"It could be anything. Maybe the guy liked kinky sex, and she didn't go along with it."

"It could be. I never thought about that. I asked about pornography, and she said no, but the way she shook her head —maybe it was something like you're saying."

"So, you don't think there is anything to her collecting the life insurance?"

"Nah, she was too matter-of-fact about it. And if you

think about it, it really is pretty normal, especially since there was a prenup and the limits in the trust."

"But it's ten million dollars. And the timing of it."

"It could just be their ages. You're behind me a few years. I'm thinking differently these days. But what I think might be worth looking into is anything that we can find around the time the policy was bought."

"That was seven years ago."

"So, figure the time they applied, the underwriting process, health exams. I'd say seven years to six months after it went into effect."

"What do you think we should look for?"

"Anything financial that sticks out. I don't know what we can get on that front, but we need to sniff around. That and anything material in Elby Salter's life and the family as well. The old man and his brother."

Derrick pulled into a spot in front of Fred Baylor's office building.

"I'll get on it as soon as we're done here."

I held my breath passing the smokers outside the entrance and nearly banged into Fred Baylor. Head down, he was tapping on his phone as he exited the elevator.

If anyone looked like they were going to throw up, it was him.

"Uh, what's wrong?"

Derrick said, "We need to speak with you."

"Uh, I can't. I'm on my way to see, uh, see a client."

"Can we go up to your office?"

"No, no. That won't work."

"There's a Starbucks in Waterside we can go to."

"I'd rather not. Like I said, I have a meeting to go to."

Derrick said, "We can do this downtown if you'd like, in an interview room."

The color drained from Baylor's face. "That's not fair. I didn't do anything."

I pointed to an empty picnic table. "Why don't we step over there for a quick chat? It's out of the sun."

Derrick and I sat opposite Baylor on concrete benches. It was hard on my ass, but the cool felt good. Baylor kept his head down.

"I know I didn't tell you everything, but you got to understand what a fool she made of me."

I said, "Enough of a fool to go out and kill Elby Salter?"

"I couldn't do something like that."

Derrick said, "You told Detective Luca you were home the night Elby Salter took a bullet to the head."

"Yeah, that's where I was."

"You told me that you remembered because it was a Tuesday, and you overdid the drinking while bowling the night before."

He nodded.

"And you were home the entire night?"

"Yeah, just watched some TV and went to bed."

Derrick said, "It's time to come clean. Where were you that night?"

"Home. I swear I was. You have to believe me."

"We would, but we have this little problem—one of your neighbors saw you drive off that night."

"What? How could they?"

"You didn't count on someone taking out the trash seeing you, did you?"

"It wasn't me."

"Come on, Mr. Baylor, we have an eyewitness."

"I can explain."

WE WERE at our neighbors for a barbecue. Other than the baptism, we had stayed to ourselves, believing, as most first-time parents did, that we had to protect Jessica from catching something. It was a small gathering, just the childless neighbors and one of their parents.

I liked Phil and Marlene; they were regular people. Phil's dad, Marty, was there. At ninety-two he was an inspiration. He had a better memory than I did and walked almost two miles each day.

Mary Ann showed off Jessie like the little princess she was. My heart surged with pride as Jessie kept smiling. After charming our hosts, we headed to the lanai.

Phil's dad said, "Frank, come sit over here by me."

I glanced at Mary Ann. She nodded approval. I settled into a cushioned chair next to Marty with my glass of wine.

"Tell me what's going on at the sheriff's office. I haven't seen you since right before that serial killer escaped."

"That was a close one. You know, don't tell anybody, but if these guys just disappeared, they'd have a better chance of getting away with it."

"You know, I was in the navy with this guy, I think his name was Bruce or Brendan. He was older than me, and he was a homicide detective, like you. Anyway, one night we were on night watch together, and he told me that if someone went to another city and killed someone they didn't know, and there were no witnesses, he'd get away with it."

There was some truth to that. We relied heavily on connections to track down killers. "It could be, but now we have a lot more tools to work with."

"In those days we didn't know what DNA was."

"In many ways, it completely changed the way we do our jobs."

"So, are you working on the murder of that Salter kid?"

"Yes, Elby Salter."

"How's it going?"

I couldn't say terribly. "I'm afraid I can't discuss an active investigation."

"They're a powerful family down here. Had their fingers in just about everything."

"I heard they had something to do with the land the Kennedy Space Center was built on."

"That's right. That was in the sixties, a couple of years after JFK was assassinated. It was a crazy time for the country."

"So, it's true they were involved?"

"Oh yeah, it got a lot of press and goodwill. Nobody could say nothing to them after that."

"I guess they deserved it."

"They certainly needed it back then. They had a kid that stirred up a lot of trouble and embarrassment."

"Florence, Elby Salter's aunt? The one who disappeared?"

"You ask me, she didn't just vanish. She was either sent away or put away."

"Really? I heard the poor woman had mental health issues."

"Is that what they call it these days? To me, she was nothing more than a pedophile."

"A pedophile? What makes you say that?"

"My son would tell me not to be spreading rumors, but when I grew up if there were a couple of rumors they always turned out to be true. You know what I mean? Where there's smoke, there's fire."

"What kinds of rumors did you hear?"

"One was when she was just a teenager. She was working at a camp for poor kids, and one of the kids said something about her touching him. The Salter kid denied it, saying it wasn't her, and the next thing you know you started hearing it was either somebody else, or the kid was making it up. You ask me, the Salters went to the media to cover it up."

"That's some story."

"It is, but it's not the only one. The Salters provided a whole lot of money for kids' programs out in Immokalee, and there was a big dustup about her having sex with a kid who couldn't be more than twelve."

"Were charges filed?"

"She was brought in and questioned, but it was dropped. It was her word against the kid's, and I remember the lawyer said in the paper that the family put the kid up to it to get money from the Salters."

"And nothing happened?"

"I don't think it was more than a month when the news broke that the Salter kid went missing."

"I understand there wasn't much of an investigation into it."

"It was in the papers, but then it disappeared. The Salters probably pushed the story out of the news."

"And nothing was ever heard about her?"

"Not that I know of. That's why I say they had a hand in it somehow. They are a powerful lot. They could've found her, if she really was missing."

"This might sound a little crazy, but you've seen a lot down here. Do you think the Salters are part of some group that runs things behind the scenes?"

"You mean a secret society, like the Illuminati?"

"Something like that."

"It's possible. There are five or six families that seem to have their hands in everything."

"Like who?"

"The Hamlets, the Wests, and the Binghams."

Those were the men in the pictures in Chadwick's office.

## 27

DERRICK STOOD AS SOON AS I CAME BACK INTO THE OFFICE. "You never told me what Annabelle had to say."

"She said there were rumors about her husband's aunt, but that's all it was. Anytime her name came up, the conversation moved away from her."

"It was forty years ago. I don't see the connection."

"Unless we find something else, we should take a look at the possibility Elby was involved in a secret group of some kind."

"That sounds like something out of a movie."

"I know, but you should watch this documentary I saw about these groups. I can't remember the name, but search for it on Netflix. It'll change your mind when you see the names of people connected to these groups."

"I don't know about all that."

"When I asked Annabelle about it, she didn't deny the possibility. In fact, she said that no matter what was going on, Elby went to a meeting on the fifteenth of every month."

"Cindy Baylor said the same thing, didn't she?"

"Yeah, we have to look into it."

"Where were the meetings held?"

"She didn't have any idea."

"We have to grill Chadwick about it."

"No doubt. I have a hunch on a couple of men who may be in the group."

"Who are they?"

"There were a couple of guys in a picture hanging in Chadwick's office. Those same men were in the newspaper a couple of weeks ago breaking ground on a new hospital out east."

"Who are they?"

"Hang on a second." I flipped through my Moleskin. "Robert Hamlet, Michael West, and Marshall Bingham."

"You want to go see them?"

"Not yet. I'm going to call Chadwick. Why don't you run a search and see what you come up with on these gentlemen?"

It surprised me that Chadwick picked up my call so quickly. I half expected him to tell the receptionist he was in a meeting.

"I trust you are well, Detective Luca."

"All is well, Mr. Salter. How are you?"

"Good, but busy. How can I help you?"

"I understand that Elby and you attended a meeting on the fifteenth of every month."

"I wouldn't call it a meeting, but we get together monthly to play poker."

"Poker?"

"Yes, a couple of us play Texas hold 'em. It's not high stakes or anything like that."

"How long have the games been going on?"

"It's a long-time tradition."

"Does your father attend?"

"Uh, yes, most times, if he is up to it."

"Who else is in the group?"

"Oh, there's a bunch of us."

"I'd like a couple of names."

"I realize gambling may not be legal, but it's a recreational gathering. I'm not sure what you're after, Detective."

"Would some of the other people be Mr. West, Mr. Bingham, and Mr. Hamlet?"

"Not Mr. West, but the others usually come. How did you know that?"

"What is the purpose of these meetings?"

"It's a social gathering. We play cards and talk."

"If that's all it is, then tell me why it is that Elby made it his business to be there each month, no matter where he was. I understand he flew back from vacations several times to make the meeting."

"Elby was Elby. I can't answer for his motivation."

"Since your brother's passing, is the meeting still taking place?"

"Yes. As I stated earlier, it's a tradition."

"Where do you meet?"

"It varies month to month."

"Give me an example."

"It could be at one of the member's homes or a country club."

"Members?"

"It's a figure of speech, Detective."

"How does one get to play? I like to play poker. Could I join in one night?"

"Oh, I wish you could, but we're fully committed at the moment."

"But what about Elby's spot?"

"It's been filled already. I'm sorry, but I'll keep you in mind."

He was using schoolyard tactics. I thanked him and hung up.

———

THE MEN I asked Derrick to check into were from families that mirrored the Salters. The Hamlets had extensive dairy and produce farms in Wisconsin and owned a bank and farmland across Florida. The Binghams were largely into retail and had put up three of the largest shopping malls south of Orlando. The West family were developers, both commercial and residential.

I sat on the bowl and thought things over as I coaxed a pee out. What was the connection between these men? Each of them fed us the same line about playing poker each month. It was a passable reason, but you didn't fly back from vacation to play cards with your pals. Elby wouldn't even cheat on his wife on the fifteenth. More than a card game was happening at these congregations.

There were questions needing answers. How many people attended? Were they all men? How did someone get in the group? Was it a secret business group? Trying to keep their dealings within a small circle made a lot of sense, and there were countless examples of businesses conspiring together to fatten profits and reduce competition. Is that what it was? Or was it a higher-level thing, like the Bilderberg Group, where they tried to control public policy?

We needed to check into the political connections the Salters and the others had. Were they influencing or bribing lawmakers? Would this end up in Tallahassee or Washington?

Zipping up, the thought that this was something perverted

swept through my mind. Was this a sex-oriented gathering? A group of spouse swappers or people into S and M practices? Or worse, pedophilia?

After splashing water on my face, I headed back to the office. The thought that a group of successful people could possibly morph into the worst scum society has ever seen sickened me. What a world for my daughter to grow up in.

Derrick was sitting on the corner of his desk reading a document. "You're not going to believe this, but there was a complaint filed against Elby Salter seven years ago."

"Okay. You going to tell me for what?"

"Sex with a minor."

**28**

———————

"Are you shitting me? Sex with a minor? What happened with the charge?"

"The complaint was withdrawn. I pulled the file, and the mother said that her kid had been lying about what happened."

"What's the woman's name?"

"Christina Matthews."

"And this was seven years ago?"

"Yeah, December 11, 2012 was the date on the complaint."

"We need to talk to this woman. Where is she living?"

"I'm tracking her down."

"What, do these Salters have a genetic defect or something that attracts them to kids?"

"If this is true, it's really fucked up."

"I'm starting to wonder if the group that meets on the fifteenth revolves around some twisted sex thing with children."

"You think so? That's a lot of people, and all of them are prominent."

"Up in Jersey we cracked a porn ring that had a couple of CEOs in it. One of them was on CNBC all the time giving advice. I'm telling you, the longer I'm on the planet, the more I'm convinced you never really know anyone."

"You're probably right, but with a couple of exclusions. I'm pretty sure I know you, Mary Ann, Lynn, and my parents, pretty much inside out."

"I'll give you that, but a lot of time people see troubling signs in others, and for whatever reason, push it aside. That's why we have more mass shootings than we should."

"We live in a world where anything is possible. Especially in our business."

"As they say, life is stranger than fiction. Look, you stay on this Matthews woman. I'm going to visit Annabelle and see what she has to say about this."

---

ANNABELLE WAS ATTENDING a luncheon at the Naples Grand Beach Resort. The hotel was at the end of Pine Ridge Road, next to the parking for Clam Pass Beach, where a body was discovered a couple of years ago. The details of the case passed through my mind until I remembered I'd been diagnosed with cancer in the middle of the investigation.

The lobby here felt swanky, like a New York City joint. I liked the open bar area that was anchored by a grand piano. I headed toward the ballroom area, stopping across from an entrance that read Save Our Turtles. Annabelle was spending her time on lesser-known charitable organizations.

A stream of women exited the affair. Annabelle's red dress was hard to miss; it wasn't flashy or sexy, but it shouted determined. Her smile disappeared when she saw me sitting in a club chair. She pecked the cheek of the lady she was talking to and nodded toward the lobby.

We settled into low-backed chairs whose comfortability was just above walking on hot coals. I didn't want anything more than water. She ordered a club soda with lime and said, "I didn't expect you so early."

"You never know how much traffic is going to be on Pine Ridge. How was your lunch?"

"Good. We're raising funds to expand our sea turtle program. Once you explain how important the mission is, people get on board."

"You put the gating around the turtles' beach nests?"

"Yes, that's a good part of what we do. We also organize sweeps of the beaches to remove plastic bags and patrol the beaches at night to make sure poaching isn't occurring."

A server set our drinks on the table between us.

She had the time and money, but I was thankful for people like her. They could spend their time and wealth on self-indulgence instead of helping defenseless turtles.

"It's good of you and your friends to help."

"We do what we can."

"I need to ask you about something that just came to light."

She looked at me as she sipped her drink.

I lowered my voice. "A criminal complaint was filed against your husband in late 2012 for sex with a minor. I assume you're aware of it."

"It was dropped."

"What do you know about it?"

"As far as I know, the girl made up the charges, and that's why it was dropped."

"Did you know the mother of the girl, a Christina Matthews?"

She took another sip to consider a response. "Not really."

"Is that a yes or a no?"

"She was one of Elby's dalliances."

"Your husband was accused of sexual impropriety with the daughter of one of his girlfriends?"

She pursed her lips and nodded.

"Do you believe the charge was revenge based? Something along the lines that Elby may have been ending the relationship, and Ms. Matthews was unable to accept that."

She shrugged.

"What did he tell you about it?"

"He didn't say much, just that it wasn't true and that lawyers would sort it out."

"The timing of the charge is close to when you bought the insurance policy. Was this related?"

"Getting the life insurance being related to the Matthews charge?"

"Yes."

"No."

"What can you tell me about Christina Matthews?"

"I'd really rather not discuss her or the affair with Elby. It was a long time ago, and I didn't know her other than her sleeping with my husband."

"I understand. Can I ask you if you knew a friend of your husband by the name of Sue or Susan?"

"Do you have her last name?"

"I'm afraid not."

"If it was a recent relationship of Elby's, I wouldn't know who she was. I tired of obsessing over what he did, deciding he wasn't going to change and that it was time to live my own life."

"I understand."

"I don't think you do. Nobody understands just how challenging it was being married to him. If that's all the questions you have, I'd like to get going. I'm due at the museum in under an hour."

The way she said "challenging" signaled it was more than his girlfriends that upset her. What was it?

"I have just one more line of questions. I understand Elby liked to play poker."

"Poker? Not that I know of."

"I thought he played with a couple of men on the fifteenth of every month."

"That wouldn't be possible, as Elby always had a business meeting on those nights."

"What business was involved."

"He didn't talk much about work with me, but he once told me it was master-planning sessions."

"Master planning?"

"Yes, important, high-level stuff."

"And you're sure he didn't play poker."

"I've known him close to thirty years, and I never saw him play or express interest in cards, or any gambling, for that matter."

## 29

---

CHESTER'S FACE WAS PUFFY. "HOW WAS YOUR VACATION, sir."

"Oh, it was great, Frank. Have you ever been to Italy?"

Frank? The sheriff was relaxed. "Just once and only Rome."

He patted his belly. "Great country. We ate and drank our way up, down, and all over the place. It was amazing. I didn't get the whole thing about Venice, but Florence, Rome, and the Amalfi Coast, geez, it doesn't get prettier than that place."

"Sounds like a wonderful time."

"It was. But all good things come to an end, they say. So, update me on Salter."

"We've got a few lines we're pursuing. We finally tracked down the woman who had filed the sex-with-a-minor case against Salter."

"It was pulled, though, so be careful with it."

"Yes, sir. She's out in California: Newport Beach." I didn't tell him that she wasn't married, which didn't fit what we knew about Elby's philandering.

"Just be careful. The Salters haven't been pressing, and I don't want them starting."

"Seems unusual they aren't pushing for a solve."

"They don't want the publicity. You mentioned something about a couple of civil cases."

"Yes, we discovered a series of civil suits against Elby Salter that were settled and sealed."

"Interesting, but sealing an agreement could just be the family trying to discourage nuisance suits."

The settled suits appeared like nuisances to me, but I didn't want to get into it with him at this point. "It could be. We're going to dig around a little, and see what we learn."

"Be discreet, Frank."

"This may sound strange, sir, but have you ever heard of a group of powerful, wealthy families, like the Salters, working together?"

"Working together on what? Business interests align themselves all the time."

"I can't put my finger on it, but I'm talking about a secret group that conspires behind the scenes."

"Don't hit me with a conspiracy theory, Luca."

"It's just that there's no doubt a set of powerful men, including Elby and his brother, Chadwick, get together monthly and try to disguise it as a poker game. If there's nothing nefarious going on, why lie about it?"

"What makes you believe the gathering is illegal?"

"Nothing concrete at the moment."

"Then make sure you act accordingly. Things are quiet around here, and I want it to stay that way."

***

"How was the sheriff?"

"Besides gaining a couple of pounds, he was his usual, cautious self."

"He didn't shut anything down, did he?"

I shook my head. "Let's go over these lawsuits again before we try and see anyone."

Derrick opened a file, separating three sets of documents. "The first one was filed on July 17, 2014, by a Paula Whiting. It alleges that Elby Salter defamed her reputation, seeking damages of five million dollars. It was settled and sealed on August twelfth. That's not even a month later."

I thumbed through the Whiting papers. There was more information on a roll of toilet paper. "What's next?"

"Patricia Corning filed against Salter February 9th, 2015. She claimed to have gotten food poisoning at South by Southwest, a restaurant owned by Salter. Corning claimed that she had to be hospitalized and that the episode caused her to lose her desire to eat and that she suffers a multitude of nutritional ailments as a result. She was looking for three million."

"That restaurant is still up in Fort Myers. I never heard anything bad about it. What's the last one?"

"Lisa Daly sued Salter back in September of 2016. Daly bought a home in Collier Isle, a community that Salter developed in 2015. She claims that the home had high levels of radon, causing her premature arthritis and exposing her and her daughter to levels that cause cancer."

"Didn't they get the house checked when they bought it?"

"Or you could put a system in for like two grand to take care of the problem."

"These are bullshit suits. That's what they are."

"No doubt, but you think it's because they're super rich? And maybe they get the cases sealed to keep them private, to prevent other people from trying to sue."

"That's what Chester said."

I almost got sunburn from Derrick's smile. "He did?"

"Yep. Don't let it get to your head. Chester may be good at assessing, but he offers a big fat zero in the solution category."

"I wonder what other counties may have. It might be worth checking into Lee County."

"It might be better off checking into some of the other high-profile folks down here. See what kinds of suits are filed against them in comparison."

"That's a good idea, Frank."

"Maybe, but instead of that, let's look into these women a little. See what we find."

**30**

---

Derrick hung up the phone and stood. "Frank, they found Elby's car."

"Who found it?"

"Customs was doing an export inspection on a container of crushed cars and ran the VIN number."

"What port?"

"Tampa."

"They put a hold on it?"

"Yeah, the inspector said they issued a seizure notice."

"We're going to have to get forensics to go over it."

"Man, this is the break we've been looking for. There's bound to be something the techs can find."

"Let's hope we don't get into some territorial bullshit with Homeland Security over custody."

"Maybe we ask the sheriff to get involved. He might be able to short-circuit this."

"A homicide always takes priority. As long as this isn't part of a giant smuggling ring that the feds are watching, we should be okay. But I don't want to waste time getting our hands on it. Let's get Chester involved."

"I'll get the details to him."

"Where was the car going?"

"China. They declared it as shipment of scrap metal."

"Who was doing the shipping?"

"A company called Sunshine Scrap and Waste. They're out of Sarasota."

"Go see the sheriff."

I plugged Sunshine Scrap and Waste into Florida's Secretary of State web portal. I scrolled to the business formation documents. It was owned by Liberty Enterprises LLC, based in Orlando.

My heart raced when the ownership of Liberty Enterprises populated. It was an entity called Hamlet Family Holdings. Could it be the same Hamlet family that Robert Hamlet was part of?

I POPPED the DVD we finally obtained from CVS into the player. I fast-forwarded to 8:50 p.m., then slowed it down. A steady stream of people moved in and out of the store.

At 9:04 p.m. I looked twice and jabbed a finger at the pause button. A guy who looked like he had a stick up his ass was approaching the front doors. I zoomed in. It was him—Fred Baylor.

I hit play. Baylor went inside. Nine minutes passed. Fred Baylor waddled out with a small white bag in his hand. It was all I needed to see. I ejected the tape and went to my office.

"Looks like Baylor was telling the truth."

"He was at CVS?"

"Yep. A couple of minutes after nine, which jibes with the time the neighbor saw him leave."

Derrick laughed. "I've heard a lot of excuses, but an itchy asshole? That's the new number one in my book."

"It's no laughing matter when you get a hemorrhoid attack. I had one a few years back."

"Why didn't he just say so? 'I had to go and get Preparation H for my butt.' That's all he had to tell us."

"I never said anything for a long time either. It's not something you share with everybody."

"I guess so."

"He wasted a shitload of our time. If he'd told us everything from the start instead of frigging dripping it, I could've taken a week off."

"Isn't that obstruction?"

"Not exactly. Not coming clean and lying are two different things. If the DA charged everyone who lied to the police, we'd have to build a zillion prisons. The distinction is if you are lying to protect yourself or someone. Baylor jerked us around, but that's about it."

"It'd be nice to have an example made of someone, to make people think twice."

"Amen. Look, I'm going—"

Derrick's phone rang. He answered it, putting a hand over the receiver, he whispered, "It's Christina Matthews."

I popped out of my seat.

"Hold on, Ms. Matthews. Detective Luca would like to speak with you."

Derrick handed me the phone.

"Ms. Matthews, this is Detective Luca. I have a couple of questions concerning Elby Salter."

"I heard he was murdered."

"Yes, he was."

"Okay."

Okay? Instead of "that's terrible?" "I understand you and Elby Salter were in a relationship."

"We were."

"How long did that last?"

"Less than a year."

"You filed a complaint claiming that he had engaged in a sexual act with your daughter."

"Sexually inappropriate behavior is what I believe the charge was."

"Okay. Tell me what happened."

"I can't."

"What do you mean, you can't?"

"I signed a nondisclosure agreement preventing me from discussing the case."

"Did he pay you to keep quiet?"

"I can't say anything."

"Why would you agree to be silenced? It's your daughter, for God's sake."

"Look, she was traumatized by, uh, everything, and it would have prevented us from moving on with our lives."

I wanted to ask her how much money it took for her to check her morality, but said, "Is there anything you can tell me about the case?"

"I'm sorry, but I can't."

"What about Elby Salter? What can you tell me about him?"

"It seems to me that you know what kind of man he is."

I spit out a thank you and hung up.

"Salter paid her to keep her mouth shut."

"She wouldn't tell you anything?"

"No, she signed an NDA. I bet that's why she's out in Newport Beach. He probably wanted her and her daughter as far away as possible."

"This charge was out there, and people had to know. I know the lawyers shut it down, but if it was real, I can't imagine it being the only time he stepped out of line. Pedophilia is a mental illness; these creeps don't do it just once."

"No doubt. The question is, was this a real transgression by Salter or something made up? Did the daughter crave attention? Did she not like her mother dating him and couldn't find a way to break them up? Or did the mother concoct the entire thing to get money out of him?"

"We should start with digging into Matthews' background. Let's see what's out there on her."

"That's the place to start. She said something to me when I asked her about Elby. She said that I knew what kind of man he was. Was she telling me he was a sex offender or just that he liked going around screwing different women?"

"If he is a pedophile, maybe he was killed by one of his victims or their family."

"Could be. Or maybe he was done in by one of his own. Someone in their secret group or his family to avoid embarrassment, to shut him down."

<hr>

"FRANK, look at this adorable dress I bought for Jessica today."

Mary Ann held up a pink and white dress with lace trim.

"It's nice. It looks too big though."

"It's not for now. Probably around ten or eleven months. It was so cute, I couldn't pass it up."

How many times have I heard that phrase in the last year? "I like it, but since there's only one of us working these days, we have to keep our spending in check."

"It's only one dress, and it was on sale."

Ah, another timeless qualifier. "How was her playdate today?"

"Oh, it was great. Jeannine set up a little splash pool, and Jessica loved it."

"Was it fresh water? I don't want her catching something."

"You're such a worrywart, Frank. What, do you think I'd let her play in dirty water?"

"You know, with this Salter case leaning toward an ugly place, we have to be careful watching over Jessie."

"What are you worried about now?"

"It may be that Salter was killed because he molested a child."

"Oh my God. Those sickos never do it just once."

"I know. There was a charge against him that was dropped, but we found a couple of civil cases that just don't make sense."

"How so?"

"Three woman filed suits against him, looking to get money. One said she got sick living in a house the Salters built, another one said he defamed her reputation, and the last one was over food poisoning at an establishment Salter owned. The cases were all settled and sealed, so we can't get at the particulars without a court order."

"And you think it has to do with sexual impropriety?"

"I don't know what to think. But I want both of us never to leave her alone with anyone, and as soon as she is able to understand, we have to make sure she knows there are sick bastards out there. She needs to know that no one can touch her, and that if she thinks something is off, she has to tell us."

It was impossible getting to sleep. The thought that something could happen to my Jessie scared the shit out of me. Did we live in a world where a powerful person could hide his disgusting acts using money, lawyers, and the courts? And even if Salter wasn't guilty of sex with a minor, he was part of some group that appeared to have their own secrets.

I knew what time it was. It was time to take off the gloves.

**31**

———

"You have to be sure Bingham is home, Derrick."

"He is. I confirmed it with a call, told him I was a property appraiser and could reduce his taxes. He bit right away. I don't blame him, he's paying fifty-eight thousand a year."

"That's insane."

"Has to be some place, probably the penthouse."

"Some apartments on Gulf Shore Drive are worth over ten million."

"That's crazy, for an apartment?"

"Go in at eleven sharp. If you get delayed, call me. We got to make sure they don't talk to each other."

"Got it."

"Text me when you're done with him."

"I'm leaving now. I'll sit in Venetian Village's parking lot if I'm early."

Robert Hamlet tried to dodge speaking with me, but the threat of having him come downtown worked, as it always did. I didn't want Hamlet and Bingham to know we were talking to each of them separately. Let's see how their stories lined up without preparation.

Hamlet Family Holdings offices were on the fourth floor of a building just off Park Shore Drive. The confines in amenities were steps above the Salter's business quarters but by no means luxurious. The low hum generated by a floor full of people just about covered the classical music playing in the background.

I waited in a conference room whose window over-looked the traffic on Route 41. On the table a map of housing plots was littered with notes. I tried to see where the development was located when the door behind me opened.

Hamlet was a big man with the beginnings of a drinker's nose. Tieless, he wore a wedding band and a white long-sleeved shirt. We shook hands.

"Detective Luca, Bob Hamlet. Good to meet you."

His hand was soft. "Thank you for seeing me."

He took the only armchair at the table, and I sat across from him.

"You wanted to talk about Elby?"

"Yes, I understand you are part of a group that gets together monthly."

"Yes, a couple of the boys like to play poker. I'm not much of a player, but some of the others think they're playing the World Series of Poker."

"How about Elby Salter? Was he one of those who took it seriously?"

"Indeed. He told me several times he wanted to try to play professionally."

"That's a whole other league. How much are the blinds when you fellows play?"

A hesitation. "Nothing big."

"Five bucks?"

"Yes, sometimes ten."

"Sounds like a fun time, but I didn't come here to ask about poker."

Hamlet smiled.

His grin vanished when I followed with, "I wanted to ask you about Sunshine Scrap and Waste."

"What about it?"

"Elby Salter's car was found at the Port of Tampa in a container bound for China."

"Really?"

"And the company sending it thousands of miles away was one of your businesses, Sunshine Scrap and Waste."

"I don't understand what any of this has to do with me."

"How did Elby Salter's car get there?"

"I wouldn't know the answer to that. I could ask my management team to look into it."

"We have to know how and when Sunshine Scrap got its hands on Salter's vehicle."

"I'm certain it is all explainable. Sunshine receives thousands of vehicles a year, from a multitude of sources: insurance companies, other scrap dealers, repair shops, and individuals."

"What do you do with the cars?"

"We recover as much precious metal as we can out of them."

"Like the catalytic converters?"

"Yes, that's the first thing they remove because of the palladium, but there are precious metals on the circuit boards, and even coins are recovered. Then, what's left is smelted."

"Why China?"

"We can't do that here; it's just too costly. We take the converters off beforehand—they're accessible."

"Who crushes the cars?"

"If they're not already condensed, we do it."

"When someone brings in a vehicle, what paperwork do you require to prove it's not stolen?"

"We pay next to nothing for these cars. There's just not a reason to steal a car and then sell it to a junkyard."

"I understand you can get up to five hundred for a car."

"If it's running, that seems reasonable."

"To an addict, that's a lot of money."

"I see your point. But Sunshine Scrap has been around for decades, and almost every vehicle comes from a commercial source."

"We're going to need to speak with whoever received the car."

"I understand. I'll make sure the documentation is ready for you."

"Someone is on the way there now." I looked at my pee-pee watch. "Should be there any minute."

He shifted in his chair. "Oh, do they know he's coming?"

"He's a she, and I have no idea."

"Oh. Okay."

It was bullshit, but I loved playing with him. Was that a bead of perspiration forming on his lip?

"By the way, I don't want the news we found Elby Salter's car to get out. You and your staff are not to breathe of word of it. Understand?"

"I'll instruct them accordingly."

"Good. Now, your family has a lot of business interests down here, don't they?"

"Why, yes. We've been here for generations and built significant holdings of farmland and a bank or two."

*A bank or two.* Like it was a kid whose mother asked how much candy he ate: *I had a Tootsie Roll or two.*

"Do you partner with the Salter family?"

"We've worked on several projects together over the years."

"Maybe I'd recognize them. Which ones?"

"We're a privately held company, and as such, prefer keeping our activities confidential."

"That seems at odds with the photo I saw in the *Naples Daily News* on the groundbreaking for the hospital."

"Sometimes we need to let the community know we are there for them. But, that said, there are enough crazies out there that it's usually better for us to keep our heads down."

"I imagine you knew Elby Salter quite well."

He shrugged. "Not as good as you'd think. He was kind of private. Well, I guess we all are. Aren't we?"

"What do you know about the charge against him concerning sex with a minor?"

His red nose whitened. "He said it was unfounded, but whether he did or didn't is beside the point, since he's gone now."

"Do you have daughters?"

"Me? No, three sons."

"I didn't think so."

"I'm sorry. I don't understand."

"Elby Salter's murder is the point. Let me remind you that hiding or fabricating information or evidence is obstruction of justice."

He was well groomed, but the stench coming off him, combined with the fact I'd run out of questions, meant it was time to leave, but I had one more question.

"Were you opposed to Elby Salter's efforts to build the Red Sox a new stadium?"

"Not particularly. Though, I didn't see the point of wasting good land on it."

"Why would the land be wasted?"

"Spring training facilities are a part-time business."

"So, you were against it?"

"You could say so."

I opened the car door to let the heat out and turned on my phone. There was a text from Derrick asking me to call him.

"What's up? I just got out of Hamlet's."

"You should have seen Bingham's face when I flashed my badge."

"What did he have to say about the meetings?"

"It took him a minute to stop stuttering, but he said Elby didn't really like to play poker. It was just a night out with friends for him."

"What about the betting limits?"

"Bingham said the blind was twenty dollars."

"Hamlet said it was five bucks and that Elby was nuts about poker. Even said he wanted to play professionally."

"What the hell are these guys hiding?"

It was a great question.

## 32

"MARY ANN! KEEP YOUR EYE ON JESSIE. I GOT TO JUMP ON my laptop."

"What's going on?"

I headed to what used to be an office but was now a repository for Jessica's toys.

"Just got the report from forensics about Salter's car. I can't read the frigging thing on my phone."

"Shush, Frank."

I turned on my HP, rolled a chair over to the desk and sat. I read the summary twice. Three specimens of unidentified fibers and several hairs were recovered. Traces of blood were discovered, but no other bodily fluids were found.

I flipped to the detail. The car's roof was cut off to gain access to the passenger compartment. The seats had been removed. Trace elements of bleach were found on the dashboard and side interior panels. The technicians believe the vehicle had been cleaned with a type of wipe, such as Lysol or Clorox, in an attempt to remove blood and DNA.

Blood matching the victim's was found on the console and dashboard. The trace amounts of blood were mixed with cleansing agents from the wipes. There was a tiny drop of unadulterated blood on the radio control unit. It was Elby Salter's as well.

Simple cotton fibers were found in the car, typical of the type used to make T-shirts. Two were dyed red, and one was white. The fibers were believed to have come from the same garment. Further analysis may clarify an origin country or possible production facility.

The most interesting finding were the hairs collected from the interior of the vehicle. Four hair samples were attributed to Elby Salter, but there were a pair of others also recovered. Both hairs were lightly curled and dyed black, matching the hairs found on Salter's body that didn't belong to him.

The back of the SUV also contained some of Salter's hair, but that was it.

None of the four tires or the undercarriage of the vehicle had any dirt particles worthy of testing.

What did this mean? There was no question there was an attempt to sterilize Salter's car. Was it just one person who abducted Salter, was in the car, killed him, and dumped the body? Or were the hairs from someone who only dumped the body?

It would have to be a highly coordinated operation if it involved more than one person, increasing the risk factor. I never leaned in that direction, but this felt like something a group of powerful people could easily pull off.

I was troubled by where the body was found. Most killers attempt to hide corpses, weigh them down underwater, bury them, or leave them in a difficult place to access. And more than a few whackos put them in freezers.

It was depressing, but what was I hoping they'd find? That the killer left his business card behind?

Mary Ann came in. "Did you get anything?"

"Not much. They found a couple of hairs that match the ones we found on the body. Whoever did it tried to clean things up, but there was plenty of Salter's blood."

"Sorry."

"It's okay. We'll get who did this. Where's Jessie?"

"Sleeping in her swing."

"She loves that thing."

"I know. You got to call Phil, and thank him for the wine he brought over."

"Oh yeah. I'll call him now."

---

"HI PHIL. HOW ARE YOU?"

"All is good, Frank. What's going on?"

"I wanted to thank you for the wine. You didn't have to get me a bottle."

"No problem. We liked the bottles you brought over for the barbeque. We never had Spanish wines before, and they were good."

"I'm glad you liked them. I thought they were good for the money, especially the ones from Ribera del Douro. They're not expensive."

"I don't know how good the one I got you is. It's from Corsica."

"Corsica? I never even knew they made wine there."

"Me either, but Marlene and I went to dinner at this little French place, Auberge, by Wiggins Pass. We didn't know what wine to order, and the owner, I think her name was Marie, suggested one from Corsica. She said she was from there and that their wines were good."

"I know that place. I thought she told me she was from Northern France."

"No, she's from the island of Corsica. It's right next to Sardinia. Sounds like a great place to visit."

"Maybe one of these days."

"We should try to plan it."

"Not with a baby. How's your dad?"

"He's good. Obsessing over the landscaper right now, but he's good."

"He's a tank. I love him. Tell him I said hello, and thanks for the wine. I'm interested to see what kind of grapes they use in it."

Corsica? I tried to recount the conversation with Marie Redoux. My memory wasn't as good as it was before getting shot up with chemo, but usually I would forget something entirely. Details, like where a person came from, I didn't mix up. Or had I?

I dialed another number.

"Derrick. It's Frank."

"Hey, how you doing?"

"Look, you remember that French woman Salter was dating, Marie Redoux?"

"Yeah, the one we saw at that restaurant off Imperial?"

"Yes. Didn't she say she was from Northern France?"

"I think so. Yeah, some place by Le Havre."

"That's what I thought."

"What's up?"

"One of my neighbors told me that she was from Corsica, an island off the southern coast of France. It's closer to Italy than France."

"Maybe her family came from there."

"I guess so, but Europeans, they don't move around too much, and Corsica is so far away from where she told us."

"Corsica. Every time I hear that, I think of the movie *The French Connection*."

"It's not what it was, but there still are crime organizations with their roots in Corsica."

"They can't be involved in this."

"Why not?"

"What are you saying, Frank?"

"I'm not saying anything. I'm just processing the information as it surfaces. I'm going to revisit Marie Redoux, see if she lied and why."

## 33

———

Derrick was reading when I walked in.

"Frank, I did some digging."

"On what?"

"Marie Redoux. There wasn't anything in the system with the same last name. Well, there was, but it was a guy from the Ivory Coast."

"The French used to run that country before they got their independence."

He held up the documents he'd been reading. "So, I went to Interpol and the French National Police, and bingo, the family is full of bad actors. They even have their own gang run by an uncle of Marie's called Lucien Redoux." Derrick flipped a page over. "This report Interpol sent over said they're connected to Unione Corse, the syndicate that ran the heroin trade between Marseille and America."

"That's the gang they made *The French Connection* about."

"They're into the usual stuff, drugs and prostitution, but here's the interesting thing. When the drug trade ended in the seventies, they moved in a big way into money laundering but also into contract killings."

"Is there anything on what their MO is?"

"Nothing signature, but a shot in the back of the head screams contract killing to me."

"Likely, but it's easier to shoot someone from behind."

"No doubt, but there's a lot of cold-blooded bastards out there."

"Is there any connection to a crime organization in the States?"

"There wasn't any mention of it."

"If they don't have any connections here, they'd have to send someone over. It's risky, if the hit man is unfamiliar with how things work here, but it goes a shitlong way in the anonymity department."

"You think they'd send someone over to kill Elby?"

"A long shot but not impossible. Get a list of all their known associates, run them against passport control. Let's see if any of them have taken a trip to the States recently."

"Start a month before Salter was killed?"

"Make it two. Dealing with Dwyer made me realize just how patient some of these nutjobs can be."

## 34

___

I slammed the phone down.

"This is bullshit!"

"What's going on?"

"That was Chester. He told me to stay away from Christina Matthews."

"You hardly got anything out of her."

"He doesn't know that, I think."

"How'd he know we were talking to her?"

"Salter's lawyer, Gerey. He called Chester and told him we were pressing for information that was protected by a nondisclosure."

"They're worried. That means there's something there."

"No doubt. It just pissed me off to no end though. Instead of trying to see what is there, Chester wants to shoo us off."

"We can ask a judge to unseal it, can't we?"

"We could, but we would need probable cause that the information in the agreement is central to a crime."

"But that's the whole point—it could be, right?"

"Exactly. Chester is acting like everyone else around here, protecting the almighty Salters. It's total bullshit."

"What are we going to do?"

"What can we do? We got to be careful. This case is a frigging mess. The last thing we need is Chester barking up our ass."

"You think the sheriff knows something?"

"I certainly hope not. If I find out he's protecting somebody, I'm out of here faster than the people going for food samples at Costco."

"I'm right behind you."

---

THE BISTRO WASN'T full despite the ten-dollar entrée special they had for diners seated by six. Redoux dropped a menu she just collected from a table of gray hairs when she saw me. I loved my job.

She took a step toward me.

"Bonsoir, monsieur, I'll be right with you."

"Take your time."

Before I had a chance to get comfortable in a chair, Marie came out of the kitchen. She banged the heels of her shoes as she walked. Was she ginning up courage, or was she that confident? I caught a whiff of garlic and oil as she approached. Escargot?

"Would you like a menu?"

"No, just here to talk."

"We're busy and—"

"Sit down."

She pulled a chair out. "What about?"

"Where are you from?"

"France."

Her accent's allure had vanished like a Florida puddle.

"It's a big country. Exactly where?"

"Corsica."

"How come you told me it was up in the northern part of France?"

"I did?"

"Yes, you certainly did."

"Most people don't realize or even know where Corsica is. It's easier to say Northern France."

"It's easier to lie is what you mean. You were very specific, telling us you were from Fécamp. I don't know much about France, but I'd say more people heard of Corsica than Fécamp."

"Is it a crime in America to misspeak on your origins?"

"Not unless you're attempting to sidetrack an investigation."

"It was an innocent mistake."

"Your family has quite a history in France."

"I don't understand."

"I believe you do. Your uncle Lucien leads a Corsican criminal enterprise. Doesn't he?"

"What is the meaning of all this?"

I couldn't tell her that I was trying to figure that out.

"I have a business to run."

"You have a daughter, don't you?"

She shifted in her chair. "Yes."

"And how old is she?"

"Fifteen."

"Were you aware that Elby Salter was accused of sex with a minor?"

The lack of surprise confused me. "No."

The front door swung open, and a couple came in.

Marie stood. "I am sorry, but I must get back to work."

I sat in the Cherokee thinking. She had an affair with Elby, admitting it was difficult for her to face the end of it.

She called him three times the day before he was killed. Why? She claimed it was about a bottle of wine. That didn't jibe. They weren't going out any longer. Why spend the money to call an ex-boyfriend from France? Was it the act of an irrational lover? Was she even in France?

We had a woman who lied to us, who may have been so obsessed over the breakup of her relationship that she went overboard, a woman who had family who were in the contract-killing business.

It was a stretch, but she also had an underage daughter. A daughter in the same age range who had made the charge against Elby. Did something happen to her?

## 35

———

ROSANNE ROBERTS LIVED IN A BEAUTIFUL ASSISTED-LIVING facility called Tuscany Villa that was close to Lely and felt like a fun place to live out the string. Inside the pastel-colored main building, someone was playing the lobby's grand piano for a handful of residents. The pianist was playing "As Time Goes By." Did anyone realize the irony?

I was shown to a lounge with a real bar. A couple of seniors were making the most out of an afternoon cocktail, and my date was one of them. Roberts bounced out of her chair like someone half her eighty-four years. She had small hands and a broad smile.

"Would you like something to drink? We call it happy hour; the drinks are free."

"No thanks, but feel free to indulge."

"I've had my gin and tonic already. One's my limit."

Hoping the wine I drank had the preserving powers that gin seemed to have, we settled into chairs around a card table.

She took off her glasses. "As a journalist, I'm curious to know how you found me."

"It was easy. I Googled old editions of the *Naples Daily*

*News* and looked at who was covering the local beat when Florence Salter went missing."

"You know, I've learned over the years that a reporter, the good ones anyway, operate like detectives do."

"That's true. If you want to find the truth, you have to dig beneath the surface."

She smiled. "And you're looking for this old spade to help brush some dirt aside?"

I liked this lady and wondered if she and Phil's dad would get along. "Any information you can share on the Salter family would be helpful."

"Well, there's a lot to cover. They were one of a couple of families that shaped this place we call paradise and made what some would consider obscene profits doing it. Now, the *News* had an unspoken muzzle when it came to writing about them. They had friends on the editorial board, and the managing editor made it clear the way they influenced how the town was developed was a good thing."

"Meaning not turning Naples into another Miami?"

Pearl earrings bouncing, she nodded. "No reporters like being told what or who to write about, but he was right. They had a lot of power, but it was all wielded behind the scenes, which bothered a lot of us. It appeared that the county commissioners rubber-stamped projects, despite objections from the public."

"Do you think there were payoffs being made?"

"I sniffed around some but could never uncover any graft. It was more like the commissioners were good, local people, but the growth outpaced their abilities. People like the Salters, who were successfully managing large business empires, were seen as white knights. They knew how to run things, and it took the pressure off the county board."

"Do you think there was an understanding or agreement

between families like the Salters to control not only the growth but the moneymaking opportunities around here?"

"I'm sure there was something like that—to share the pie they were baking."

"Do you think the cooperation extended into anything illegal?"

"I don't get the question. Their business interests seemed to be aboveboard."

"What about removing an obstacle?"

"Oh, this is getting interesting. I had forgotten you were a homicide detective. I never heard any rumors about something like that."

"Tell me about the Florence Salter situation. I understand she had been accused of sexual misconduct with a minor."

"When I hear something once, I learned to be skeptical and look for confirmation, but when the second incident surfaced, I thought there had to be something to it."

"And was there?"

"Sadly, it seemed that the allegations could be true. The paper covered the charge, and when it was dropped, made sure the news got out, as it, frankly, should have. If there's a thing the news media gets wrong, it's the failure to cover a retraction as well as the original story. But in this case the charge looked to be true."

"What do you remember about it?"

"The Salters were and still are active in the philanthropic scene, and they had funded a youth center for the underprivileged kids out east. A young boy, I think he was twelve or thirteen, said he had a sexual encounter with Florence Salter. When word got out, the boy's mother found out, and she filed charges."

"What makes you believe he didn't make it up?"

"It surfaced when he started telling his friends what

happened, and kids, well, they talk. A volunteer found out and confronted the kid, who got his mother involved. A reporter I worked with, a fellow called Benny Goshen, poor guy passed ten years ago, he talked to a couple of the kids and found two others who said she'd performed oral sex on them."

"Kids tend to be unreliable, don't they?"

"Naturally, but Benny said both kids gave him the same location where they claimed it happened and the dates and times as well. He checked into it, and she was there at those times. And the thing that was interesting was the kids were not friends with each other and came to the center at different times."

"Why didn't this get reported?"

"Benny went to the editor, but they said it was unsubstantiated, and the original charge had proven to be false, etcetera, etcetera. They said to hold off until more evidence surfaced. But, a couple of weeks later, she disappeared."

"What do you think happened to her?"

"I think she took off. She was finished around here. Maybe she knew other charges would surface, and she'd go to jail."

"Do you think her family helped her disappear?"

"I'm sure they did. She was an embarrassment to them. The Salters are a proud lot and were probably happy to see her go."

"Didn't anyone try to find out what happened to her?"

"We covered it at first, but the fact was, there was nothing to follow. She had to leave the state, and the paper wasn't going to pay for us to look around the country. Who knows where she could have gone? She could have even left the States. They had enough money to get her a new ID and move her anywhere."

"You think she could be locked up somewhere in an institution?"

"Unlikely. She was a bright woman. I couldn't see her staying in a place like that. Unless they drugged her somehow."

"Do you think they could have arranged for her death?"

"Kill their own daughter? I don't know, but I guess it's possible. Those types of people don't get fixed. It's an illness, if you ask me. And if she's in Timbuktu, she's probably doing the same thing and eventually would get caught and exposed for who she is."

"Elby Salter was her nephew and about the same age as the kid who made the charge against her. Do you think it's possible he was molested by his aunt?"

"Of course, it's possible. I'm sure there was plenty of opportunity for her to do so, and Elby had to view her as an authority figure."

"That's what I was thinking. Assuming it did happen, it's possible that Elby was damaged by the abuse and turned into someone who pursued sex with kids himself."

"And some parent found out about it and killed him."

Roberts must have been a good reporter; at eighty-four she still knew how to piece a story together.

**36**

———

THE RED SOX WERE SPREAD ALL OVER THE FIELD. A GROUP was fielding grounders, others were stretching in the outfield, and on the sidelines pitchers were throwing to catchers. Weaver and I were the only two in the owner's box. It wasn't as swanky as I expected, but it was a spring training facility.

"This is a nice place to watch a game. I'd come more often if I could sit up here."

"Anytime, Detective. You let me know a day before, and I'll make sure it happens. Bring your family if you want."

"Thanks. I appreciate that. I may take you up on it. My partner follows the game more than I do."

"Just let me know."

"Thanks, I will."

"Good. Let me ask you something. It's got nothing to do with Elby, but it's a law thing."

"Sure, fire away."

"There's this guy. He's a fan of the team, and I'm pretty sure he's been stalking me."

"What makes you believe that?"

"He's showing up almost everywhere I go. I'm ninety-nine percent sure he followed me home after Tuesday's game."

"Do you feel threatened by it?"

"It's happened a couple of times when I was playing, but it was mostly kids or women hanging around. It's kind of spooky this time because we've been getting nasty letters about not signing Blair to a contract."

"From one person?"

"We think so. I mean, there are plenty of cranks unhappy about this and that, but this seems different."

"Is he making threats in the letters?"

"Not exactly."

"Give me an example."

"He just says that if we don't sign Blair, he knows it's my fault. And that there are a lot of accidents that happen every day and not to make a mistake because he won't want anything to happen to me. It's kind of a meandering drivel into how the Sox have to have Blair, and if we don't get him the world is going to end."

"I don't like the way that sounds. Can you identify this person?"

"Oh yeah, he's at every game. He has season tickets for spring training. Guy was here even when I was playing." Weaver laughed. "Either he's working for Blair—maybe he's getting a piece of his contract—or a screw has come loose."

"I'll put a call into a buddy of mine, Tim Winters, as soon as we're done. He's with the Lee County Sheriff's Office. What time's the game today?"

"One o'clock."

"If this nut is coming here—"

"Oh, he will be."

"Then I want you to call Winters when he does. You're going to have to file a stalking charge against him though.

But we'll arrest him, bring him in, and see if we can scare him to his senses. Are you good with that?"

"Absolutely. But I don't want him arrested in the stadium."

"They wouldn't do that. Winters will grab him after the game. He'll keep it low-key. Take down his number."

"Okay, I really appreciate it. What did you want to ask me about?"

"You and Elby spent a lot of time together, right?"

"Mostly right here. Our relationship revolved around baseball. He really loved the Sox, and if he were still here, we'd be moving to new digs in Collier."

"Why did the deal for the move collapse?"

"Elby drove it. There was a lot of opposition from business and fans. Once he was gone, it fell apart."

"Why? Who pulled the plug?"

"The Salter family trust, as I understand it, assumed all or most of Elby's interests, including the land for the stadium. They pulled out."

"Did Chadwick make the decision?"

"I honestly couldn't say. We, the team, tried to save it, but in the end, we decided fighting them and others who wanted us to stay put just wasn't worth it. And look, this place isn't so bad, is it? It's a helluva lot newer than Fenway."

Watching a stream of players jog around the perimeter of the playing field in the sun did make for a pretty sight.

"Let me ask you something more personal about Elby. Did you ever see him make an overture to a young girl?"

"What do you mean?"

"A few years back a complaint was filed against him, charging him with having sex with a minor."

"I knew about that, but it was dropped. Apparently, it was just some ex-girlfriend fishing for money."

"Well, she seems to have gotten it."

"Excuse me?"

"A settlement was reached with the mother of the girl who made the accusation. She signed a nondisclosure agreement in exchange for what must have been a nice chunk of change."

"Are you saying there was something to the charge, and he paid her off to keep it quiet?"

"I'm trying to piece the puzzle together. There were also three other civil suits filed against him that were settled and the details sealed by the court."

"And you think it had to do with something deviant?"

"My job is to explore every possibility, and sometimes it gets ugly."

"What, that Elby was a pedophile or something? And he paid people off?"

"I can't say with certainty, but the possibility exists."

"But why would these women need to go to a court?"

"Not sure, but it may be as simple as to show that they were serious."

He put his hands on his head. "You got me reeling. I don't know what to make of all this."

"Think about anything along those lines. Any behavior that seemed out of place?"

"The only thing I can think of, and it wasn't out of place, it's just because of what you're saying, was that Elby always made sure he was here when they had events for the players' kids."

"Anything seem suspicious in retrospect?"

"Not that I can think of right now."

"You roll this around, and let me know if you think of anything."

**37**

---

Derrick picked up the phone, talked for a moment and said, "Frank, there's a woman reporter, Roberts, on the line."

Had she remembered something, or had I turned into an alternative to bridge and cocktails?

"Hello, Ms. Roberts. How are you?"

"I couldn't be better. Listen, after you left, I started to think about the entire thing. There was a lot going on back then."

"The allegations against Florence Salter?"

"No, not her. You mentioned the possibility that a group of the movers and shakers were acting together to achieve their means. It's true, but I think I heard you intimate the possibility that they'd taken a dark turn."

"I can't say much, but it's safe to say when they get together, they're not playing Scrabble."

"They should. It keeps me sharp. It dawned on me how there really wasn't any competing visions. Everyone got behind whatever proposal it was, and that was that. But I remembered there was this man, Dennis Harding; he was an East Coaster and owned a couple of parcels of land on Gulf

Shore Boulevard by Venetian Village. Harding had inherited the land and moved to Naples to develop it."

"Harding? The name doesn't ring any bells."

"I'm not surprised. You were riding bicycles when he was here. Harding intended to put up a bunch of high-rise residential buildings on the land."

"I guess he succeeded. I always thought it was kind of strange that that's about the only place where there are tall buildings clustered together on the Gulf."

"He did, but there was quite a battle. There was a lot of resistance to Harding's plan, but he had the approvals for the project; they were grandfathered in when his daddy owned it. He was taken to court, but he prevailed. He moved back to West Palm, but construction of the first tower began."

"That's interesting."

"Here's where it gets interesting. The iron framework for the first tower was up, and Harding came in for the groundbreaking of the second building. Now it could just be my imagination running away, but that night he was killed in a car accident on Alligator Alley. He hit something that had fallen off a truck, lost control of his car, and was found dead."

I WAS LYING on the floor playing with Jessie when Mary Ann said, "Frank, your cell is ringing. It's Derrick."

"I'll be right back, pumpkin." I kissed a chubby leg and got up.

I took the phone from Mary Ann. "Keep your eye on her."

"What's up?"

"Guess who was in the States?"

"I love you, brother, but I'd rather be playing games with Jessie than with you. What are you talking about?"

"Two of the mugs in the Redoux crime family flew into the States. One arrived in Miami just four days before Salter was shot, and another guy flew into Atlanta nine days before the murder."

"Holy shit. We may be onto something. Did they fly back out?"

"No record of them leaving. They could have scooted over the border into Mexico or Canada. There's limited enforcement, especially on the way out."

"You have pictures of the men?"

"Passport photos, but they're a couple of years old."

"That's okay for now. See if the French authorities have any recent photos of the two of them. But first, get those pictures over to the witness who said he saw something that night."

"I already called him. I'm in the car heading over to see him now. I'll be there in a couple of minutes"

"That's the way to do it."

"You want to take a ride? I can wait there."

I did, but he seemed to have things under control. "It's all yours; just be careful. One photo at a time. Give him enough time to mull it over, and don't tip him off as to who the guys are."

"Got it."

"Call me as soon as you're done with him."

"Okay. Hold on, I forgot to tell you that Marie Redoux, she was in France when she said she was."

"It could be that she planned it that way to have an alibi."

"I couldn't see her doing the killing anyway. If she had a role, it was in hiring someone or getting a family member to do it."

"But if it wasn't money, she'd need something compelling for her family to jump in. The Corsicans may be rough, but they're not a Chicago street gang, killing for the fun of it."

"True."

"Let's see what your witness has to say first. Good luck."

I stepped back into the family room trying to process the likelihood Elby Salter was killed by French assassins. Mary Ann was holding both of Jessie's hands, helping her to try walking.

I got on my knees. "Look at you, Jess. You're walking."

"She's doing a lot of it on her own."

"She's going to be walking soon. I can't believe how big she's getting."

"I'm thinking of going back to work next month. What do you think?"

"We can use the money, but I'm having second thoughts with everything. Who can we trust to watch over her?"

"Charlene said she used a service, and they were wonderful."

"A service? So, we're going to leave our kid with a complete stranger? I don't think so."

"They're professionals, Frank. They have resumes and references we can check."

"Look, can we not have this conversation right now? We can afford to have you home with Jessie for a few months more."

"It's not the money, Frank."

"Then what is it?"

"I'm getting a little antsy staying home. That's all."

I wanted to say that we could trade places, but I understood where she was coming from. Mary Ann was a good detective and was used to having things come at her like a summer rainstorm.

"We'll put a plan together, don't worry. Maybe in two

months we could do two days a week to make it easier on Jessie."

"I've given it a lot of thought, Frank. I figured three half days are better to start with. Human Resources said they could work it out, and I think that's the best approach."

I wanted to complain about her unilateral approach, but I liked the idea. "That's a good way. She'd only be alone with someone for a couple of hours. You'd be back before you knew it. But can't we do two days to start with?"

"Let me see how things go with her the next week or so."

"Okay. Sounds good."

I checked my phone. Nothing. Why hadn't Derrick called? He said he was minutes away. Had something happened? To him? I dialed his number.

# 38

---

Derrick was downstairs getting his required marksman work in at the shooting range. Sucking the last drops of coffee out of my travel mug, I wondered if he had a Dunkin' coffee for me somewhere. I hoped so. I had come to depend on that rather than the cafeteria's industrial java.

I was reading an article on interpreting body language when my phone rang.

"Luca, homicide."

"Hi, Detective Luca. It's Ron Weaver."

"How are you, Ron?"

"Good. I wanted to thank you for getting the detective from Lee County involved."

"Tim Winters, he's a good man."

"Well, he arrested this guy, and there was no commotion at all. It was like, one, two, three, and he was in the back of the car."

"I'm glad it worked out for you."

"I was worried. You know how it would look having a fan arrested. But I don't think more than a handful of people in the parking lot knew what was going on."

"That's good. This guy will leave you alone now. He probably just needed a good scare."

"I know, but I'd prefer not to press charges and turn it into something big."

"You can drop the complaint in a week or so. Let him stew for a while."

"That's a good idea. I'm going to do that."

Derrick walked in, without coffee.

I said, "That's good, Ron. I've got to get moving."

"Okay, but I was thinking about what you said about Elby and anything weird."

"Did anything come to mind?"

"It's probably nothing, and I feel like I'm pissing on his reputation . . ."

"It's okay. Whatever you say stays here. What is it?"

"Well, we were at a game one day, and he said that some woman looked like his girlfriend Marie's, kid. Then he said, except the daughter had a set of unbelievable knockers for a kid."

"Did he say anything else?"

"No, that was kind of it."

"Did he regularly make those kinds of comments?"

"Not any more or less than most men."

"Most men?"

"I should have said athletes. I'm around a lot of them, and well, they can get a little rough."

"Did Elby seem excited when he spoke about Marie's daughter?"

"I didn't pay much attention to him when he said it."

"Was there anything else you remembered?"

"No. And I got to say, if you didn't bring the subject up, I probably wouldn't have even made the connection."

"I understand. But do me a favor, will you?"

"Sure, what do you need?"

"When some jerk makes a comment like that, don't let it pass. Say something, or stick a damn sock in his mouth."

"Oh, yes, I definitely will. Have a good day."

I slammed the phone down.

"What's going on?"

"That was Weaver. He said Elby had made some comment about Marie's kid at the ballpark."

"What did he say?"

"Something about the girl having big breasts."

"The guy's a frigging slob. He probably was a pervert."

"I don't know what to make of it. These shitheads shooting off their mouths. I'd like to ram my fist down their throats."

"It's not worth getting upset about. Relax."

It was easy for him to say. He didn't have a daughter to worry about. "I'm going to take a leak."

Sitting on the bowl I realized emotion wasn't going to solve anything. What did the information Weaver passed on really mean? Was it possible that Elby Salter had crossed the line with Marie Redoux's daughter? Had he sexually assaulted her? Was this a confirmation he was a pedophile?

If there was any truth to the extrapolation, we had our motivation. It wasn't Marie acting as a spurned lover but as a mother hell-bent on revenging the violation of her baby. It was a powerful, logical reaction, if that is what it was.

As my pee began to flow, I realized that coming from a family comfortable with crime, it would have been easy for Marie to arrange for the killing. No need to hunt behind the scenes with shady characters to find someone that would not only do it, but do it right and keep their mouths shut about it. She could go to people she knew and presumably trusted. It was simple, and frankly, too convenient. Did family members get a discount on contracts for murder?

Or had it been something that was out of her control? Had the news of Elby's transgression, if there was one, reached her family, and they had taken matters into their own hands? Maybe Marie tried to stop it but ran against the twisted honor thing criminals like to invoke to explain their behavior.

Zippering up, I wondered why the witness hadn't identified either of the French men as the one with Elby Salter the night of his murder. Could his memory have failed him? Eyewitnesses were problematic—always sure of what they had seen, until they weren't.

If it were members of a French crime family who did it, they could have been wearing disguises. According to Interpol, they were experienced contract killers, used to taking every precaution available to avoid detection.

Where the hell were they now? Once someone entered the country, keeping track of them was almost impossible. If they'd come in, made the hit on Salter and left the country, we'd never catch them.

Drying my hands, a spit of bile hit the back of my throat. I remembered what the instructor in the detective training course had said about catching perpetrators: If someone went to a town hundreds of miles away, had never been there or knew anyone there, committed a crime and left, that there were slim chances of catching them.

In this case we might know who did it, but they were five thousand miles away, protected by a foreign government. Making a case against them would be paddling around the world in a leaky kayak.

## 39

———

THE NOONTIME TRAFFIC GOING NORTH ON 41 WAS AT A virtual standstill until I passed Immokalee Road, when I cracked the window and stepped on the gas. I couldn't wait to hear what she would have to say. Turning into the parking lot, I knew this was a critical point in the investigation.

The outdoor tables were empty. I opened the door to Auberge, scanning the square dining room. Four tables of two, and six at a round table, were eating their lunch, but there was no Marie.

A smiling waitress held up a finger as she carried a bottle of white wine to a table. She plunked it into a wine bucket and hurried over.

"Good afternoon. How many today?"

"I'm not here for lunch. I need to speak with Marie Redoux."

"Oh, she's not in today."

"Is she out sick?"

"No, she said something had come up."

I was going to her house but asked, "Will she be in tomorrow?"

"I don't think so. I'm usually off tomorrow, but she asked me to make sure I came in."

"Okay. Maybe I'll see you for lunch tomorrow."

"Can I tell her who came to see her?"

"I'm with a wine distributor, nothing big, just wanted to have her taste something I think she'll like. I'll come back, thanks."

Where the hell was she? Had she run, believing we were closing in? As a precaution, I called Derrick to let him know I was heading to Marie's house. It was a protocol I usually didn't follow.

---

MARIE REDOUX LIVED IN ESPLANADE, a new community that required every homeowner to join its golf club. I drove alongside the golf course, past a dozen tennis courts and made a turn, passing the new rage in active lifestyle, pickleball courts. I didn't get the need for pickleball, but then again, I didn't get golf either.

It looked like the homes on both sides of Terrace Way had water views. I tried to remember what the price points were. The houses were large. With water views, they had to be around a million and a half.

Marie lived about halfway down the block in a tan one-story home. A pair of royal palms stood like sentinels on each side of the driveway. There wasn't a car on the street. I walked up the drive toward a swaying tiger palm tree that obscured the door.

Wondering what kind of views the home had, I rang the bell. No answer. I paired the next ring with a couple of knocks. Nothing. Maybe she was sitting on the lanai. My shoes sank in the wet grass as I walked along the side of the house.

The kidney-shaped pool was screened in. I walked toward the water and looked back. No one was in the covered part of the lanai. The house was empty.

I climbed back in the Cherokee and headed to the office, wondering where Marie Redoux was.

---

"Did you catch up with Marie?"

"Nope. She wasn't at home either."

"Strange, but it could be legit."

"That's why I'm not jumping to any conclusions, in spite of the fact that I'm an Olympian gold medalist in the sport."

"Funny."

"Look, get Customs and Border on the phone. We need to get an alert out on these French guys. I want every pair of eyes looking for these two, especially along the Canadian border."

"Why do you think they'd go to Canada rather than into Mexico?"

"Millions of Canadians speak French, especially in Quebec, where the majority does."

"Oh yeah, Lynn and I went to Montreal, and we couldn't believe it was the main language up there."

"There's a long history between France and Canada. I'm worried they won't get challenged if they cross over."

"I'll get on it."

"And I want footage of them coming in at Miami and Atlanta. Get the video of what they look like now and show it to the witness. See if he can identify either one of them."

"I'm on that one already. I filed the requests this morning."

"Good."

Derrick picked up his phone as I stared at the pictures of the men we needed to find. Jacques Redoux was thirty-six with a closely trimmed beard and wavy black hair. Was it dyed? He was first cousins with Marie. My guess he was probably in charge of the operation. He had flown into Miami, while Pierre Bouchard had arrived at Atlanta's airport.

Bouchard had a sharp nose and a small scar on his chin. Was this the triggerman? He didn't look like the man in the sketch the police artist had drawn. In fact, neither man bore any resemblance to the drawing.

I was as concerned as every other citizen by the loss of privacy caused by the increasing number of cameras being deployed. But boy, did I wish I had some video to work with.

This felt like some Hollywood movie—foreign killers sneaking into the country to avenge an atrocious act. It'd sell tickets, but like most of the garbage coming out of the industry, was it far from reality?

It bothered me that Marie hadn't shown up at work, wasn't home, and wouldn't answer her phone. Maybe it was a coincidence, but you know how I feel about coincidences.

**40**

---

Marie answered when Derrick called the restaurant at 10:30 a.m., excusing himself for calling the wrong number. I was waiting at the other end of the parking lot, and when he texted she was in, I hustled to Auberge's door. It was locked.

I knocked on the door repeatedly, wondering if she would bolt out the back door. Finally, Marie appeared, carrying a tub full of cutlery. She frowned when she saw me, set the silverware on a table and opened the door.

"So, it *was* you yesterday?"

"What tipped you off?"

"There aren't any wine distributors who look like George Clooney."

It was childish, but I liked the compliment; it made the me feel like I still had it. Or was Clooney's hair getting more salt than pepper too?

"There are questions you need to answer."

"Really? I'm very busy, and if I prefer not to?"

"I'll have you brought to the sheriff's office for questioning. It shouldn't take more than three or four hours, if they have a room available."

Her eyes narrowed. "What do you want with me?"

"Truthful answers."

She crossed her arms. "I've been truthful."

"I'm not here to debate with you, ma'am. Shall we sit?"

She stepped aside. "I don't have a choice. We have a large party booked for lunch. Make it quick."

Empty restaurants had the same sadness that spending your birthday alone had. A celebration was waiting to happen but no participants to get it off the ground. I took out my Moleskin and settled into a wobbly chair.

"I understand you had a couple of visitors from France."

A look flashed across her face. Was it surprise or puzzlement? "Visitors? I don't understand."

"Your cousin Jacques flew into Miami."

"He did? When?"

"Just a couple of days before Elby Salter was murdered."

"I told you before that I was in France when that happened."

"Yes, I know. We verified it with Homeland Security."

"Then why are you questioning me?"

"I don't believe it is a coincidence that your uncle heads a Corsican crime family known for contract killings and that two members of that syndicate arrive in sunny Florida just days before Elby Salter ends up dead. That's what's troubling me."

"I have no idea about this coincidence, but who is the other person? You said two members."

She was honest or playing a good game of dumb by asking about the second man. "Pierre Bouchard."

"Never heard of him."

"That may be true, but it's not surprising. I'm sure you know that contract killings need levels of deniability to be effective."

"Detective Luca, the mystery you are weaving here may be fascinating in the cinema, but I have a restaurant to run."

"Did your uncle, Lucien, send a couple of his henchmen to kill Elby Salter?"

"Why would he do something like that?"

"Because you asked him to."

"I did no such thing."

"Or he decided on his own to right a wrong and to protect the family honor."

"And what honor are you speaking of?"

"Your daughter."

She leaned in. "Keep my daughter from your hallucinations. She has nothing do with any of this."

"You know what I think? I think Elby Salter crossed the line somehow with your daughter. I'm not saying she had anything to do with him. It wasn't her fault. But there are signs that Elby Salter had a fetish for young girls."

"Are you through? Because I have nothing further to say, and I must prepare for lunch. If you have proof to back your wild ideas, present them. Otherwise, I'm asking you to leave."

She stood, shoulders back and lips tight.

"Thank you for your time, Ms. Redoux."

On the drive back to the office, I kept replaying her responses. Was it her European background that muted the reading of her body language? She was protective of her daughter, but who wasn't?

I needed more evidence, something that she couldn't deny, maybe even something that would let me talk with the daughter. I'd love to question the kid, but I didn't want to put her through anything unless I had rock-solid proof it would help the case.

On the way back to the office, Derrick called.

"Frank, how did it go with Marie?"

"Nothing to report. She denied knowing about the French hoods coming here. She even said she had no idea her cousin was here, claiming she was in France at the time."

"A good alibi, but it falls to shit if this is a conspiracy."

"I know, and what bothers me is she's in France to see her family. What are the chances she doesn't know her cousin is here? It would be one of the first things people would talk about. She lives in Florida, a cousin flies into Miami, and it doesn't come up?"

"I don't buy it either. She had to know. I don't care if it's a second cousin. Lynn had an aunt in from Ireland, and this woman wanted to know if we knew her second cousin. And the guy lived somewhere near Chicago."

"She also shut me down as soon as I brought up her daughter. She didn't want to talk about her, telling me not bring her in to things."

"You asked about the kid and Elby Salter?"

"Yeah, I framed it delicately, but she still flipped out. I don't know if there is anything there or not, but I need to find out."

"We will. Look, I have digital copies of the video footage from both Hartsfield and Miami airports. I've got my laptop, and I'm going to see the witness. Let's hope he can identify one of these men as the guy he saw the night Salter was killed. If he does, we're on our way."

I appreciated Derrick's sense of urgency. "That would be a good way to start the weekend."

"I'll call you and let you know. If there's nothing there,

then I'll see you tomorrow. It's a one o'clock game. I'll swing by around eleven thirty, okay?"

"Perfect. Let me know what happens with the video."

**41**

———

We made our way through a crowd of kids and seniors to our seats. More than half the people were decked out in Red Sox jerseys and baseball caps. Spring training had become a mainstay for snowbirds and locals.

The attraction wasn't only the weather: the action was closer, the players were more willing to engage, and the tickets cost much less than the regular season.

"These are great seats, man."

"I wish Weaver could have gotten us into the box, but John Henry, the owner of the club, is using it today."

"You ask me, these are better; we're closer to the field."

"Weaver said these seats are for the scouts in the organization."

"Next year we should bring the girls out to a game."

"That's a good idea. I'll leave it to you to set it up."

"You got it. I still can't believe the Sox let Blair go."

"They did?"

"Yeah, last night, he signed with the Yankees. They gave him a ten-year deal."

"I wonder if Weaver had anything to do with it."

"He did. Him and Riley said they had a kid in minors they could wait on instead of a long-term, expensive deal with Blair."

"I remember him saying something about a player in the minors he thought would be ready in the middle of the season."

"You want a brew?"

THE RED SOX were getting shut out, and the fans were chanting the name Blair in unison.

"You hear these guys? It's only the fourth inning, for God's sake. There's plenty of time."

"Fans of winning teams are not long on patience."

"You're right. I like the game, but I can't imagine rooting for a team that loses all the time."

"Here comes Weaver."

As he made his way to us, a chorus of boos broke out.

"Hi, Ron, this is my partner, Derrick Dickson."

They shook hands and I said, "They take this seriously, don't they?"

"Man, you don't know the half of it. The shit hit the fan after Blair signed with New York."

A fan a dozen rows back started shouting, "You suck, Weaver. Get another job." I hiked my chin in the rowdy guy's direction, and Derrick left to quiet him down.

"Sorry about all this. We have passionate fans."

"Why don't you go up to the box?"

"You sure?"

"Yeah, thanks for the tickets. They're great."

Out of the corner of my eye I noticed a man charging up the stairs. As I turned, he flung a beer at Weaver, soaking one of his pant legs and getting some of the suds on my arm. The red in his face nearly matching the B on his hat.

He screamed, "You're a fucking idiot. We need Blair, you moron. You're destroying the team!"

He wore nothing under his Boston windbreaker, which was unzipped to his navel. Stepping between them, I put my palm on his clammy chest, which he promptly knocked away.

"Calm down and watch your language, tiger. There are children here."

"I'll calm down when this moron learns how to run a goddamn team."

"If you don't shut your mouth and get ahold of yourself, you're going to get thrown out."

"Sure, that's what this team is all about, screw the fans as long as they're raking the dough in."

Derrick sidled up to me saying, "This is your last warning."

He bore his eyes into Weaver before turning around. I wondered what was in the bulging pockets of his cargo shorts as he swaggered back to his seat.

Derrick said, "What a lunatic."

I whispered, "I think he's carrying. It looked like there was a bulge on his right hip."

"He better have a permit."

Before I could respond, Weaver said, "That's the fan your friend arrested."

"Are you kidding me? The guy was locked up a week ago, and he's making a scene already?"

"The Blair thing must have set him off."

"I don't care what might have happened, this dude needs to be on meds or locked up."

Derrick said, "It's pretty obvious he didn't get the message. He should be booted out of here."

"I don't want to cause a scene."

"It's your call, but if you don't, you're encouraging him and all the other crazies, for that matter, to do whatever they like."

"Frank is right. You can't allow this. Nuts like him will scare away the families."

Weaver lowered his voice. "I'm in a delicate situation here. The public relations people said we have to be careful dealing with discontented fans. They said it backfired on the Marlins a couple of years ago, and their attendance never bounced back."

Derrick said, "I remember that. They were even talking of moving the team out of Florida."

Weaver said, "That's right. They're still losing tons of money. There's a rumor they might be sold."

"Look, I don't know anything about marketing, but I don't want anybody getting hurt, that's all."

"Me neither. I'll talk it over with the guys in the box and see if we can get something out reminding fans on the club's behavior rules."

"Good. What's this guy's name?"

"Eugene Smick."

As the game wore on, I kept my eye on Smick. He didn't do anything but cheer like crazy as the Sox fought their way back, eventually winning the game by a score of nine to eight.

I wanted to ask Weaver if he remembered anything more about Elby Salter and Marie Redoux's daughter and went to the owner's box as soon as the game ended.

Weaver was coming down the hall and smiled. "Good game. Wasn't it?"

"I didn't think the Sox would come back. Maybe you don't need Blair after all."

"I hope so, or I'll be looking for a job."

"You'll be okay. Look, I just wanted to check again to see if you remembered anything more about Elby and Marie Redoux."

"You know, I gave it a lot of thought, but nothing came to mind. He liked her, no doubt, and I think he was upset when she broke things off with him but—"

"She broke it off with him?"

"Yeah."

"Are you sure?"

"Yeah, I'm pretty certain about it."

---

DERRICK WAS WAITING by the main gate for me. There were a handful of stragglers milling around in hopes of getting autographs.

"Weaver said Marie broke things up with Elby. That's not what she told us."

"She lied again."

"I know, but why? Could she have ditched him after he did or tried to do something with her kid?"

"Logical conclusion. But why was she calling him from France?"

"Could she have been trying to extort money from him?"

"And he refused to play along, and she had him killed."

"Exactly."

Derrick elbowed me. "There goes our friend."

Eugene Smick was walking toward a white van whose back doors were covered in bumper stickers.

"What a piece of work. He needs to get a life."

**42**

─────────

Wʜɪʟᴇ I ᴡᴀs ɢʀɪʟʟɪɴɢ ᴀ ᴄᴏᴜᴘʟᴇ ᴏꜰ ʜᴀᴍʙᴜʀɢᴇʀs, I ʟᴏᴏᴋᴇᴅ
up and admired the orange-streaked sky. Checking out the stars was also something I'd started to do. I would have to accumulate some knowledge of the planet, otherwise Jessie would think her dad didn't know anything before she hit her teens.

Mary Ann stepped through the slider with Jessie in her arms. "Where's the remote?"

"On the table."

"You have to see this. They're rioting in Paris."

The TV came to life, displaying thousands of protesters marching down the Champs-Élysées. Fires were raging near the world's most expensive stores.

"Oh my God, look what they're doing. We were just there."

"Disgusting. What set them off?"

"I heard something about raising the gas tax."

"What, five bucks a gallon isn't high enough?"

"Look, the Louis Vuitton store is all boarded up."

"The cops should use water cannons to stop them."

"Look at all the graffiti on the Arc de Triomphe."

"Those are graves they're desecrating."

The video of a line of police marching with riot shields toward the protesters was interrupted by a journalist interviewing a masked man in a yellow vest. To the right, a crowd of his cohorts were gathered.

"Look at that sign. What does it say?"

"*Liberté*. It means freedom in French."

"Holy shit!"

"Frank! When are you going to stop using foul language around Jessica?"

"Sorry, sorry—"

"Stop with the sorries. You want her first words to be curse ones?"

"I promise, okay? It's just that, remember that body that was found on the boat at Naples City Dock?"

"The one without an identity?"

"Yeah. He had a tattoo that I thought was in Spanish. It's been a while, but it could be French."

WE WERE SPEEDING along Interstate 75, having just passed Venice. We'd be in Sarasota in under half an hour. It was a long drive, and even though it violated my mantra on diligently using our resources, I was glad Derrick was with me. I said, "I always thought the dead boat guy was the triggerman. After he killed Salter, someone killed him to make sure he never talked."

"Me too. That's why I was surprised he wasn't one of the French guys."

"There could have been a third man in the operation."

"That's what I'm thinking. He could have been a local the French hired."

"Or someone the poker-playing group hired."

"I don't know, Frank."

"How did Elby's car end up in the hands of a company controlled by Hamlet?"

"I'm hoping we find out today."

A pair of trailers made up the offices of Sunshine Scrap and Waste. Small hills of scrap metal and crushed cars dotted the several acres comprising the property. Two yellow, claw-like machines were lifting cars as if they were cereal boxes, and a pair of orange shredders, fed by a tractor, were spitting out screeching sounds and strips of metal.

We stepped inside the trailer. It was what you'd expect at a junkyard. The carpet was ripped in places, and the four desks held mounds of paperwork and auto parts. A salty woman with a smoker's voice went to retrieve her boss.

Two men weaved their way to us. We shook hands with the manager of the yard, Marty Vine, and the company's lawyer, Louis Alispi.

Vine had sandpaper-rough hands and wore a white dress shirt that might have fit him twenty years ago. His mouth-piece was dressed in a blue suit and a red tie. Half the size of his client, he was nonetheless protection.

We squeezed into Vine's office, where an air-conditioning unit hung on the wall. Why someone had taped streams of paper to its outflow was puzzling as it emitted a loud hum when it ran. Through the window, a car in the grips of a machine was being stacked.

Alispi sat catty-cornered, trapping his client behind a desk piled with papers. He said, "I understand you're interested in Sunshine Scrap's acquisition of a certain 2018 Ford Explorer."

"The one that belonged to Elby Salter."

"The records we have indicate it was brought into the yard on February twenty-first."

"What time?"

"We don't record the time of day."

"Who brought the SUV in?"

"A man called Dick Simon."

"What kind of ID do you require?"

"This is a copy of the driver's license he presented."

I took the sheet of paper. "Have you done business with this guy before?"

Alispi looked at Vine, who said, "Not that I'm aware. We take in fifteen hundred vehicles a month, minimum, sometimes sixteen, or even seventeen hundred."

Derrick was better at math than I and said, "That's over fifty cars a day."

"If you say so. I just know if we get sixty or more a day, we're doing good."

Simon looked like a marine—crew cut and square jaw. He was sixty-two years old and five foot ten inches. He wouldn't need a gun to intimidate someone like Salter. His address was listed as 3874 Deerfield Drive in North Sarasota.

Derrick said, "How much did you pay for the car?"

"Five hundred and fifty."

"Five hundred and fifty dollars? Why would someone sell a relatively new car for just five hundred and fifty bucks, when it's worth thirty or forty thousand?"

Alispi said, "We cannot speculate as to the motivation of the firm's clients, but it's doubtful that the value you assigned is accurate."

"And why do you say that?"

He slid a photograph across the desk. "See for yourself. We printed this from the digital photo taken."

The white paint was blotchy. It looked like some type of corrosive had been sprayed on the SUV. The roof toward the rear had a large dent in it, and the rear window was missing. The photo raised more questions than it answered.

I said, "The car came into the yard in this condition?"

"Yes."

"And it was driven in by Mr. Simon?"

"Yes, that's what we believe."

"Believe or know?"

"We have no reason to believe anyone but Mr. Simon brought the car in."

I studied Simon's driver's license. It was hard for me to believe he wouldn't call a tow truck to move a car like this the twenty miles or so from his North Sarasota home—unless there was something fishy going on.

"What did you do with the car after it came in?"

Vine said, "Well, we strip off the parts we can sell or get precious metals out of, like the catalytic converter and circuit boards. That kind of stuff."

"Then what?"

"We crush 'em."

"The Explorer was in a container bound for China. Who ordered that?"

"We ship a lot of scrap over there. Their labor costs are a tenth of ours, and they can do stuff there that would get us shut down."

"Was there anything out of the ordinary in processing this car?"

"What do you mean?"

"Was there special handling? Was it expedited?"

"Not that I know of."

"Did you or anyone else receive any communications from the outside regarding this vehicle?"

"Outside? I don't understand."

"Did anyone from upper management or the holding company that owns this facility, or anyone from the Hamlet family call or communicate in any way about receiving, processing, or arranging the shipment of the Explorer in question?"

"I didn't talk to no one about nothing."

We left there and headed straight to North Sarasota. I couldn't wait to hear Dick Simon's story about Salter's car.

**43**

───────

It took us only fifteen minutes to get to Newton Estates, where Simon lived. His street backed up to a park anchored by a library. It was a quiet middle-class neighborhood with neatly maintained homes.

"Slow down, Derrick, but don't stop. His house should be in the middle of the block."

"That's it. The green one."

A man came down the side of the property pushing a lawn mower. "Is that him?"

"Yep, that looks like him."

"He's wearing headphones. Pull up next door."

Derrick and I spread five feet apart and approached him. Simon's T-shirt hugged his chest and shoulder muscles. The guy had the body fat of a broom stick. He stopped mowing as we stepped onto his grass, put the mower in low, and pulled his earphones out.

Derrick said, "Mr. Simon? Dick Simon?"

He stepped forward. "Yeah, that's me. What's going on?"

We flashed our badges. "Detectives Dickson and Luca from the Collier County Sheriff's Office."

"Collier County? What do you want?"

"We'd like to speak with you. Can we go inside?"

"Sure." He shut the mower. "Come with me."

The house was dark and cool. A large fish tank glowed in the family room. A loaf of bread sat on the kitchen counter next to a couple cans of tuna.

"Take a seat. I don't know what I can help you with."

We sat around a glass-topped wicker table.

"I understand you recently sold a Ford Explorer to a junk-yard called Sunshine Scrap and Waste in Sarasota."

"Ford Explorer?"

"Yes, a white, 2018 Ford Explorer."

"You got the wrong Dick Simon."

I unfolded the copy of his license. "That's you, isn't it?"

"Yeah, but the car I junked was my wife's old Gremlin. It was a 1978 and costing me more to fix than it was worth."

Derrick said, "Are you sure?"

"Of course, I'm sure." He got up. "Hang on, I'll get the papers."

Derrick rose. "Hold on, let me come with you."

"Whatever you want. It's in the den."

The three of us walked down a hallway into a den whose walls were covered in maps. I put my hand on my holster as Simon bent down and opened a drawer. He came up with a green Pendaflex file, laying it on the desk.

"Here. Here it is. They gave me a hundred and fifty for it." He held out a receipt from Sunshine Scrap.

I snapped a picture with my phone and asked, "Do you have the registration for it?"

He fished in the file. "Here you go."

Simon appeared to be legitimate. "Do you know Elby Salter?"

"You mean the rich guy who was killed down in Naples?"

"Yes."

"No. How would I know him?"

"Do you know anyone in the Hamlet family?"

"No idea. I don't even like Shakespeare."

---

"WHAT THE HELL is going on, Frank?"

"I'm trying to figure out what this means. If Hamlet thinks he can jerk us around, he's in for a shitstorm."

"You think he figured we'd take whatever bullshit they fed us?"

"They're too cautious for that. That's why they had a suit there, to make sure it didn't escalate."

"Vine is going to shit himself when we show back up."

"Let's think this through. Whoever killed Salter had to deal with his car. Rather than leaving it somewhere to be found, knowing there was going to be DNA recovered, they junked it. A pretty good idea, except the car was fairly new."

"And we saw the ATM video; the car didn't have any damage then."

"Good point. Besides who brought the car in, the question is who battered the car? The scrapyard could mangle it in seconds. But that would add to the number of people who were a part of any scheme."

"Do you think there's any chance Redoux and Hamlet are working together?"

"If they are, then, for sure, we've seen everything."

---

I TOLD Derrick to hit the siren and the lights right before we swung into the scrapyard's driveway. Vine was on the porch of the trailer before we got out of the Cherokee.

"What's going on?"

"You lied to us."

"What? I didn't lie."

"You want to do this out here?"

"No, come to my office."

We settled into the same chairs, but he didn't have his flak jacket sitting next to him.

"You told us you bought the car from Dick Simon."

"Yeah, that's right."

"Well, Mr. Simon sold you an old Gremlin, not an Explorer."

"That's impossible. The paperwork said it came from Dick Simon."

I held out my phone. "Is this your receipt?"

"It looks like it. Yeah."

"Who does it say you paid?"

"Richard Simon."

"For what?"

His shoulders sagged. "Uh, a seventy-eight Gremlin . . ."

"You want to explain what is going on here?"

"I, I don't understand. The paperwork must have gotten mixed up. Hold on a minute."

He went to the door. "Ellen! Get over here!"

Vine told her to go through all the files, that some paperwork had gotten mixed up. He had a look of concern but not panic.

"I'm sorry about all this. I hate to say it, but we're not the best organized around here."

Derrick asked, "Did someone instruct you to lose the Explorer's paperwork?"

"No."

"It's okay if they did. You just tell us. You're not going to get in any trouble. You were just following orders."

"No. Nobody said anything to me."

I said, "Are you protecting the Hamlets?"

"No, I swear."

"Are you sure? If you are, we'll find out, and then you'll be up to your ears in trouble."

"I'm telling you, the paperwork just got mixed up, that's all. We'll find it, sooner or later. You'll see."

Derrick said, "You better hope you do. And if you attempt to fabricate the documentation, our lab will find out, and you'll be thrown behind bars."

"I would never do something like that."

I said, "We're going to go back to Collier, and I want you to think this over. Maybe you'll remember something about how the papers got mixed up. If you do, just let us know. We're not interested in you. We'll give you a pass. You don't have to worry."

"I don't know how it happened, but as soon as we figure it out, I'll call you."

"Good." I pointed out the window. "Say, do you know how to operate one of those?"

"Sure, I worked one like it for a good ten years."

**44**

———————

I said, "Wow, this coffee is hot as hell,"

"When you told me you were going to be late, I nuked it, getting a coffee from the cafeteria," Derrick said.

"We interviewed a nanny this morning."

"How'd it go?"

"It's hard, man. I want to grill them like a suspect, but last week the woman cut me short and left. You can imagine the crap I got from Mary Ann."

"You got to be sure. You're talking about your kid."

"I know. I'd like to find a way to keep Mary Ann home and make some extra dough."

"Why don't you move upstairs, Frank? You've been doing this a long time, and you'd make twenty percent more."

"I can't. Management and playing politics isn't me. Besides, I love hunting down killers and working cases."

Derrick pointed to the board hanging between our desks. "Even when it feels like we're chasing our tails?"

"It gets frustrating, no doubt, but we stay on it, and sooner or later, we'll get the bastard."

"This one is frustrating."

"Remember, step back and review. The water clears up when you do it."

"So, we got the French angle . . ."

"Start earlier. We have a wealthy, influential male killed after withdrawing three grand from an ATM. We don't know if the withdrawal means anything, but robbery doesn't jibe with the way he was killed and dumped. He was married without children. He has one brother, a possible competitor. His best friend, or who he considered to be his best friend, is an ex-player and executive with the Red Sox, a team he loved and tried to move to Naples."

"He was involved in a bunch of different businesses, and with shady partners like Friedman."

"No doubt. He also liked screwing around with other women, married women. He had to make enemies, with the women's husbands, and women like Marie Redoux, who had the connections to kill Salter. Then there's the trail of lawsuits and whispers of his possible fetish with young girls."

"If it's true, it's the most compelling motivation we probably have."

"Probably, but he was part of a group of powerful men who run half the state, one of whom just happens to own the scrapyard that arranged his car to be shipped to China under the guise it was junked. A place that claims the car's paperwork is missing and whose manager knows how to operate the machinery to make it look like a heap of crap."

"And what about those meetings? The whole poker-playing charade is nothing but a cover."

"The question is, for what? Is it connected to pedophilia? Did he cross a line with someone in the group? Or could it be about a business deal gone wrong?"

"It looks like they reversed the stadium deal."

"That was Chadwick. He had control of Elby's assets."

"You think he was involved?"

"It's funny. I can't see him acting alone. Maybe it's the family thing. But as part of some group, with some stupid code, I can't rule it out."

"These are not street mobsters; they're educated. I can't see it."

"Did you forget the IQ that Dwyer, the serial killer had? I'm going to see Chadwick. Let's see what he knows."

HAVING MET with Chadwick several times and never getting to see the color of the paint they used inside was not only odd, it deprived me of information. Anytime you encountered a suspect or witness in their personal space was an opportunity to peer in a window.

It was his office again, an impersonal, sterile environment. It affirmed the understated manner the Salter family seemed to operate in, but the only thing I learned came from the picture in his office, the picture with some of the other so-called poker players. It was solid information, but what did it mean? Was this just a group of businessmen cooperating to line their pockets? Were they engaged in rigging things? Or was there an evil component to this influential group, perhaps something as disgusting as child porn?

Pushing through Southern Enterprises' door, I immediately recognized Chadwick's voice. He sounded like the narrator of a documentary. He was talking to an associate and turned toward me as I entered. He smiled, finished up with his colleague, and said, "Let's go to my office."

He flicked the lights on, and I noticed the fishing picture was no longer hanging on his wall. What did that mean?

"How are you, Detective?"

"I'm well, thank you."

"I hope we can get this accomplished in the next twenty minutes. I'm on a flight to Orlando in an hour."

It had to be a private aircraft, or he was lying.

"No problem. Two things today. I had a couple more questions, and I wanted to share some information on the investigation into your brother's murder."

He stiffened. "Okay, go ahead."

"First up, I wanted to advise you that we've located Elby's vehicle."

"Oh. I guess that's good."

He knew we'd found it. His buddy Hamlet had probably called him before we got back onto the interstate.

"Elby's Explorer was sitting in a container about to go on a ride to China."

He cracked a knuckle. "Interesting."

You learn that we find the car your brother was slain in, and that's interesting?

"What's really interesting is that the company involved in the attempt to conceal the vehicle is owned by a friend of yours, Robert Hamlet."

"That's not surprising. They probably control more than half the scrap market in the state."

"He also happens to be in the group that meets on the fifteenth, isn't he?"

"What are you inferring, Detective?"

"Mr. Hamlet told me he was opposed to Elby's effort to move the Red Sox into Collier. Why were you and Hamlet against the stadium deal?"

"It added little economic value, and combined with a higher-level profile than my family is used to, it was unappealing."

"Your brother disagreed."

"Elby followed the team like a ten-year-old and had his eyes closed. Even when he received threatening letters from fans, he kept pursuing it."

"Threatening letters?"

"That's what Annabelle told me."

"Did she or Elby let you see any of these letters?"

"Yes, Annabelle showed me one. It was very troubling. I tried to tell Elby to be careful, but he brushed my concerns away."

Annabelle had told me that Elby had destroyed the letters. Was she mistaken? "Do you remember what the letter said?"

"Something along the lines that if he didn't stop the effort to move the team that he'd regret it."

"Did you believe the threat was credible?"

"I didn't know what to make of it but thought the prudent course was to exercise caution."

There was a beep on his desk phone, followed by a voice over the intercom.

"Mr. Salter, I'm sorry to interrupt, but you wanted to know when Sue called."

"Tell her I'll call her back."

"Sue? Would that happen to be the same Sue that your brother was having an affair with?"

"Oh, no. That was Sue, Sue Mallory, she's a, a designer we're working with on a project."

"I'm interested in speaking with the Sue your brother knew. Do you know where I could get in contact with her?"

"Not exactly, but she used to work at that French restaurant by Imperial Golf Course."

"Auberge?"

"That's it." He smiled. "It was typical Elby. He was seeing the owner, and next thing you know he's involved with one of the staff."

**45**

———

"Looks like we found Elby's girlfriend, Sue."

"Are you kidding me?"

"No, according to Chadwick, who was hiding something, he said this Sue worked at Marie Redoux's bistro."

"How the hell is this all connected? We need to talk to her. You want me to call the restaurant and track her down?"

"No. I don't know how this fits, but we can't tip Marie off that we know about her. Get into the state portal and hunt her down through the employment records."

"Good idea."

"I'm going to call Annabelle. Chadwick said she showed him one of the threatening letters Elby got. But first I want to run down Hamlet for leaking the news about Salter's Explorer to Chadwick."

"He told him?"

"I'm pretty certain. They way Chadwick reacted just didn't fit."

"If they're in it together, you'd have to expect it."

"You know, you're right. I'm going to leave him alone. I

want both of them thinking we don't suspect anything. Get me the contact details for Sue."

"I'm in there now."

I called Annabelle. She was wishy-washy on whether she had actually shown one of the letters to Chadwick. She did remember telling him about them but couldn't recall showing him one. Did every piece of information in this case come prepackaged with gray film over it?

---

Mysterious Sue was actually Suzanne Lynn Bellows. Her driver's license put her at thirty-five and five foot four. Married, she lived in Meadow Brook Preserve, an older apartment complex on Old 41.

Before leaving, I checked on what the places were renting for. The midrange was fifteen hundred a month. Elby didn't leave her any money.

I rang the bell. She peered through the peephole, asking who I was. She was alone. She asked again, and I repeated myself, holding my badge up. Two locks unlatched, and the door opened. Bellows had high cheekbones and chestnut eyes that were Asian looking. Her athletic wear hugged her yoga-instructor shape.

"What's the matter?"

"Suzanne Bellows?"

"Yes."

"Detective Luca, Collier County Sheriff's Office. I'd like to ask you a couple of questions concerning Elby Salter."

Her face darkened. "Oh, come in."

The apartment was an inside one, with only rear windows and a single transom over the door. She walked me the five feet to a small kitchen table. There were flower patterns and pastels everywhere you looked. Bellows lived alone.

"I understand you and Elby Salters dated recently."

"Yes, I still can't believe what happened to him."

"How did you meet him?"

"I was a hostess at a restaurant and met him there."

"Auberge?"

"That's right."

"When was this?"

"A year and half or so."

"But he was dating Marie Redoux then, wasn't he?"

She smiled. It was a nice smile. Like most people, Elby seemed to like pretty smiles.

"He was, and it cost me my job."

"Because you got in the way of their relationship?"

"I didn't do anything. Elby flirted with me left and right, but I needed my job and was married. I brushed him off, but Marie, she fired me."

"Did you date him then?"

"No, I was married. I still am, but we've been separated since then, and it's over now. You see, my husband, he was a cop in Lee County, and it had to be Marie that told him I was involved with Elby. It was a total lie, but Tony has a temper. It ended up costing him his job, and he kept accusing me, and we couldn't get along and separated."

"Is that when you started up with Elby?"

"No. I didn't want anything to do with him, especially after denying it with Tony. He would have lost it."

"How did things start with Elby?"

"I was at opening day for the Red Sox spring training with Tony. He's a big fan, and we used to go all the time. He wouldn't take no for an answer, so I met him there. Anyway, when I was there, I ran into Elby. We got to talking, and you know, he asked me out. It was kind of funny because I only saw him because we were, like, twenty rows away, and there was all this commotion going on down below us. I looked to see what was going on, and it was Elby. Some fan was screaming at him. Elby said the guy did it all the time. Anyway, we reconnected then, and it was going good, but then . . ."

"You said your husband had a temper. Did he know you were dating Elby Salter?"

"Yeah. Tony would keep tabs on me like crazy. He accused me of seeing him the whole time and that I lied to him."

"How upset did he get?"

"Very upset, but I'd been out of the house for a good six months."

"Did he ever make any threats against Elby?"

"I thought he was following us, but Elby thought it was a Red Sox fan."

# 46

---

Beating Derrick into the office was happening less and less often. There was always something going on that hung me up, but today I was up early with Mary Ann and Jessie. I needed to dig into Sue Bellows' husband.

Derrick strolled in. "Hey, Frank, thanks for having us over last night. Lynn couldn't stop talking about Jessica. As soon as we get married, I think we're going to try to have a baby."

"You haven't lived until you had a kid, but take a year or two to do it. You're going to need the time for each other; you know, settle in as a couple first."

"You think so? We've been living together almost a year and a half already."

"Trust me on this, partner. Take your time. You're both a lot younger than Mary Ann and me. Don't rush it; you want to get this right."

"Thanks. We'll have to talk it over."

"Good. Look, this husband, Tony Bellows, of mystery girlfriend Sue, is a real winner. I spoke to my buddy Tim

Winters in Lee this morning. He said when Bellows was on the force that Internal Affairs had his number on speed dial."

"What he do?"

"More like what didn't he do? Used excessive force three times, the last time on a sixty-year-old woman he pulled over for speeding. Bellows broke her arm."

"Guys like him really screw the rest of us."

"Amen. I don't know how they get on the force in the first place. I'm going to go see him. You want to come?"

"I can't. Got to hang around for a call from Homeland Security. Looks like they may have something on our French friends."

"They tried to leave the country?"

"Not try, one of them may have slipped into Canada. They're running a bunch of videos, and I'm going to be joining in on a web video call."

"Nobody understands just how easy it is to cross over, thousands of miles and hundreds of thousands of people each and every day."

"When we deploy facial recognition systems it'll make it a lot easier."

"The privacy issues shouldn't derail it. Everybody has to show their passport, which has their picture. I'm taking off; see you later."

TONY BELLOWS SHOULD HAVE BEEN TILTED to one side from the weight of the chip on his shoulder. He had an attitude before I told him why I was there.

Bellows was five foot four inches, maximum. Why was it that smaller-built males felt the need to prove they were tough? He was dyeing his hair black, another sign of his insecurities.

His apartment was twice as large as his wife's but had less furniture than a dorm room. What it did have was a Boston Red Sox throw on the couch and a collection of Boston baseball caps spread over two shelves. I followed him into the kitchen.

"Sit where you want."

I slid a kitchen chair out, and Bellows kicked a chair out with a foot and sat. One elbow on an arm, he had a lean build that a seventeen-year-old from Brooklyn would envy.

"I understand you were with the Lee County Sheriff's Office."

"That's right. Six years of service, and they threw me to the curb like a dog over some bitch who resisted arrest."

Fifteen years ago I would have gotten into a pissing match with this jerk, but it wasn't worth it. "What are you doing now?"

"Not much, helping a friend out here and there. I'm waiting to see how the suit I filed against the department plays out."

"As I said, I'm investigating the murder of Elby Salter. I understand your wife started a relationship with Mr. Salter just before he was killed. What do you know about it?"

"Is that what she told you? She was cheating on me with him when she worked at that French place. That's when she started with him."

"Was it a continuous relationship?"

"What are you asking me for? Ask her. She's the one who was sleeping with him."

"I'm trying to get all the angles."

"There's no fucking angle but one. She was married to me but was sucking some rich guy's—"

"Hold on. Let's keep this civil, otherwise we can do this downtown."

Bellows' ears flattened. He shifted his lean to another elbow.

"We have a witness who said that you were stalking Elby Salter in the weeks before he was killed. Is that true?"

He took too long to answer. Bellows was a cop and knew something about interviews. He was calculating a response, knowing if he went down a rabbit hole, I was going to be right behind him.

"It wasn't anything like that."

"Tell me, then. What was it like?"

"I was pissed, man. How the hell would you feel? All of a sudden we're not going to get back together, and she says she wants a divorce. I'm like, trying to figure out what changed. We were working on things, even went to a marriage counselor. What a bunch of bullshit that was. Then she just says it's over. So, I followed her around, trying to see what was going on. That's all it was."

"And you followed her when she was with Elby?"

"But it was once, maybe twice."

"Where were you the night of February twentieth?"

"Aw, come on, man. You got to be kidding me. I'm a police officer."

"It doesn't matter what you were. Tell me your whereabouts that night."

"I don't know. I was probably home."

"As a former officer, you know *probably* is not going to cut it. You want me out of your hair, give me an alibi."

"I don't remember that far back."

"Would you be willing to voluntarily submit a DNA sample?"

"Are you crazy? They'll frame me in a heartbeat."

"Do you really believe we'd frame you for something you didn't do?"

"Maybe not you, but the Lee County cops? Oh yeah, you forget I'm suing them? They'd get me on something just so they won't have to pay me."

I didn't agree with his logic, but I could see how he would believe it.

"Can I use the restroom?"

"Oh, no, man. You ain't going to pull that trick on me."

He could deny me a chance to grab some DNA today, but we'd get some. Maybe there was some in an old case file. If not, I'd lift it somehow.

I left him and sent a text to Derrick asking him to get Bellows' driver's license picture to the witness.

**47**

———

I'D NEVER BEEN TO A BASEBALL PARK OR ANY SPORTS ARENA as much as I had been to JetBlue Park during the time we were trying to solve Salter's murder. Ron Weaver had arranged for me to meet with a couple of people who worked in direct contact with fans. I had a picture of Tony Bellows I wanted to show them.

It was something that needed following up on. The Boston Red Sox connection was coming up too often to ignore. The parking lot was filling up, even though it was more than two hours before the game.

A father was holding hands with two blond girls who looked to be six to ten years old. The little one was skipping like she was going to Disney World. I couldn't wait to do things with Jessie.

I heard a strange motor sound overhead. A yellow biplane towing a Geico banner was making its way over the stadium. Out of the corner of my eye I saw a white van. Was it that nutty fan's van?

The need to check it out hit me, and I weaved around two groups of fans toward the van. It was an older model, something from the late nineties. Its antenna was capped with a baseball. A pair of red socks along with 2018 World Champions was painted on a side window. Either this guy's wife was as big a fan as he was, or he wasn't married.

Circling to the rear of the van, I stared at a collage of bumper stickers. More than half were versions about keeping the team in Fort Myers:

Don't Mess with Our Team

Move and Lose

Fight the Move

Moving's Losing

I stood on my toes. Peering through the tinted back windows, I couldn't make out what was lying on the floor. Heavily tinted windows were outlawed in many states as it increased the danger for officers being unable to assess a situation. But with Florida's abundant sunshine, and the heat and wear that came with it, they were allowed.

Something on the floor looked like a small animal, maybe a dog. I knocked on the door, but whatever it was didn't move. Was it dead? Or was I mistaken? Struggling to remember the owner's name, I snapped a picture of the license plate.

Sending a text to Derrick, I nearly smacked into a T-shirt vendor just inside the entrance. It seemed that more than half the crowd was taking photos with their phones. Taking pictures of everything but seeing nothing, I thought. Then I remembered I'd been walking and playing with my phone, acting just like the people I criticized.

I made my way to the mezzanine level, where the Red Sox offices were. The club's work space was smaller than I'd expected. A cheery woman in a Chris Sale baseball shirt greeted me.

"You must be Detective Luca. I'm Cathy Burns, the Fan Service manager."

"Nice to meet you, ma'am."

"Welcome to JetBlue stadium. This your first visit with us?"

"No, I've been here before. In fact, me and my partner were here for the Yankee game."

"Great."

"You know, I thought there would be more people working for the team."

"There are, but most of them are up in Boston. Mr. Weaver said you wanted to discuss fan feedback."

Feedback? Is that today's lingo for fans vomiting their opinions?

"I realize we live in a time where many people feel the need to tell the Red Sox how they should be doing things. Fans like to complain. They've been doing it since the Ancient Olympics. Venting is okay, as long as it doesn't escalate."

"We have a passionate fan base who like to express themselves."

"I have some questions I'd like to ask about some of what you deal with."

"Sure, happy to help with anything."

"What I'm interested in are letters, calls, or people that are unusual or are repetitive to an excessive degree."

"We have our regulars. But we liken it to people who write letter after letter to the editor of a newspaper."

"Do any of the regulars do anything that a reasonable person would feel was over-the-top or crossed a line somehow?"

"Most of the fan interaction is directed at the players, and it's evenly split that we should get this player, or we should get rid of that one. And there is a good deal of complaining about the size of some contracts, especially when a player underperforms."

The majority of fans were regular people looking for entertainment. It made sense that they'd get upset with the millions of dollars being thrown at people who played a game for a living.

"I understand that the loss of Blair to the Yanks was a sore spot."

"He was a fan favorite for almost a decade and built a relationship with them. It was a business decision, and I wish I could just tell them so, but we have to be careful how we communicate the business side of things with fans."

She was like a mother protecting a badly behaved child. "Is the name Tony Bellows familiar to you?"

"Yes, how did you know?"

I didn't need to show his picture. "We ran across his name. Did he do anything that rang any bells?"

"He was upset, like many fans were, over Blair and the talk about moving the team into Collier County. You have to understand, the majority of our fans are traditionalists. The Red Sox play in Fenway, after all. It's the oldest stadium in the country. We even put in a manual scoreboard down here, just like the one in Fenway."

"Did he do anything to give you cause for concern?"

"He wrote emails every day, and one time he came up here screaming to see Mr. Henry—he owns the club."

"What happened?"

"Mr. Henry wasn't here. We told him that, but he wouldn't leave, and we had to have security escort him out."

"Did he get physical?"

"He put up a fight. When the escort guard tried to grab his arm, he shoved him into a wall. I tried to reason with him, but it ended up they needed to get three guards to get him, but that was all."

Bellows shot to the top of the suspect ladder. "Anyone can just walk up here?"

"No longer. After that incident we lock off the corridor."

"Excuse me a second." A text had come in from Derrick. The name of the owner of the van I had forgotten was Eugene Smick.

"When my partner and I were at the game with the Yankees a fan had an encounter with Ron Weaver. This man was cursing and even threw some beer at him."

"Really? Mr. Weaver didn't say anything about it."

"The man's name is Eugene Smick."

"Oh, Eugene's a bit emotional. Most of the people think he's a weirdo, but he's a nice guy. You know, one time last year my car wouldn't start, and he saw me in the parking lot and came over. I didn't know it, but lucky for me he works at a place called Bobby's Auto Service, and he was able to get my car started."

"That was nice of him."

"It was, but the best part was it had something to do the starter thing, and he told me to come straight in, and he'd replace it at cost for me. So, I called my husband and told him I was going to go down to J & C Boulevard to get the car fixed."

J & C Boulevard? That was where Elby Salter's body was dumped. But it was also an industrial area where hundreds of businesses were housed. If you were working down here and weren't in retail or tourism, there was a good chance you worked in that area.

## 48

CHESTER WASN'T HAPPY ABOUT ME PULLING IN TONY Bellows. At times Chester was a politician, while I was always a homicide detective.

"Derrick, check the thermometer."

"It's reading almost eighty."

"Nice and toasty. What time is your guy coming in?"

"He should be here in ten minutes."

"Perfect."

We peered at the video feed. Bellows had his lean on. It could be that he used to be a cop or knew that we were watching him, but his posture was as cocky in an interview room as it was in his apartment.

"How much longer you want to give it, Frank?"

"It's been forty minutes; let's get to it."

Derrick gave a quick knock on the door and we entered.

"It's hot in here, Frank."

"Oh yeah. Check on the air, will you?"

Bellows never shifted his gaze from the wall behind me as I sat.

"Sorry about the heat."

A snort was his reply.

Derrick came back in. "I lowered it to seventy."

"Thanks."

Derrick turned the video on and stated the formalities before asking the first question.

"Mr. Bellows, how did you know Elby Salter?"

"You know damn well how I knew him."

"Did you know him before your wife, Suzanne, started a relationship with him?"

"No."

"Were you upset about the relationship?"

He looked at me. "What's wrong with this fucking guy?"

"Watch your language, Mr. Bellows, and answer the question."

"Of course, Sue was my wife; she still is."

"Did you stalk Mr. Salter and your wife when they were together?"

"It wasn't stalking. I followed her because, all of a sudden, she didn't want to try and save the marriage anymore. I wanted to find out why."

"And that reason was Elby Salter, wasn't it?"

"Yeah."

"And you were so enraged by it that you shot him in the back of his head."

"Look, man, I came here voluntarily, without a lawyer. I don't need this bullshit, okay?"

I said, "After you discovered the relationship by following them, did you follow them again?"

"Just one more time. I'm pretty sure."

"Pretty sure? You wouldn't remember following someone?"

"Like I said, I followed them about two times."

"Did you ever follow Elby Salter when he was not with your wife?"

I could almost hear the whir in his head as he hesitated. He didn't need to answer; I knew he'd followed Salter.

"I don't think so. I mean, I might have followed him for a little bit after he dropped off Sue."

"Why would you do that?"

"I don't know. I just did."

"Did you ever confront him?"

"No. I would never do something like that."

Derrick asked a good question. "Did you ever follow your wife around?"

"Yeah, sure I did. She needed watching, didn't she?"

"Did you ever threaten your wife?"

"What I said to my wife is between us. It's none of your damn business."

I said, "I understand that you wanted to speak to Mr. Henry, the owner of the Red Sox."

"What's that, a crime in Collier County?"

"We were told that when you were told he was not in, you caused a scene."

"He was there. Chicken was afraid to talk to me, face the facts that him and his buddies are screwing the fans who put money in their pockets."

"You refused to leave, and when a security guard was called to help, you got physical with him."

"Fucking Kmart cop put his hands on me. Nobody puts their hands on me. Nobody."

"When you confronted Elby Salter, did he put a hand on you, and that's why you shot and killed him?"

"No."

"Would you like to reconsider that answer?"

"Look, I didn't do anything to him."

"We have a witness who gave us a sworn statement that you said, 'I'm going to kill that rich bastard.' Isn't that what you said?"

"That's bullshit. Everyone says things they don't mean. I was mad, frustrated, goddamn it! Why can't you understand that?"

"Did you say it or not?"

"Oh, man. What, are you working with those bastards up in Lee County? They had no right to remove me from the force. I was doing my damn job."

"We have nothing to do with whatever happened in Lee County, including whatever lawsuit you have against them. Did you threaten Elby Salter?"

"All right, already. I said some stuff, but that ain't no crime, and you know it. I don't know what's going on here, but I want my lawyer."

"We'll end our questioning, then. You can call your lawyer and have him meet us down here. You're going into a lineup, with or without your lawyer."

***

It took an hour for Sheldon Fisher, a lawyer for the International Union of Policemen, to arrive. The officers working for the Lee County Sheriff were unionized, something the officers in Collier County weren't. Fisher had defended and lost Bellows' attempt to fight getting booted off the force. Was he still paying union dues?

Bellows and Fisher were holed up in a private room before the lineup. We couldn't eavesdrop. Since plastic surgery to change his looks wasn't an option, I wondered what advice was being tendered by the three-hundred-an-hour suit.

After twenty minutes, Fisher stuck his head out.

"We're ready to proceed. Where is the witness?"

"Waiting in the reception room."

"I don't want my client walking past him. It will prejudice the witness."

"We're aware of tainting the results. The lineup room is just down the hall. The witness will not be brought to the viewing room until the men in the lineup are settled."

"That's satisfactory. Let's get this over with."

Usually I never liked to fill out a police lineup with officers only. I generally wanted to have at least two or three civilians standing with the suspect. In this case, Bellows had been an officer, so the ability to sniff out a cop wouldn't impact the proceedings.

The problem for us was finding four officers as short as Bellows. We couldn't and pulled two guys out of the IT department to go with one cop from the cyber and and one from the financial crimes units.

I popped into the prep room. Bellows and the others were given numbers to hang over their necks. Bellows wore number five. He'd be the last one in the lineup. Everyone was ready. I told them I'd call when we were set.

Derrick and the witness were in the darkened viewing room. I warned Fisher to keep quiet before joining my partner. As soon as I stepped in, Derrick said, "I have to talk to you as soon as we're done. Just received an interesting email."

Nodding, I hit the switch for the lineup room. The witness took a step back as fluorescent light flooded through the viewing window.

"It's okay. No one can see us in here."

"Are you sure?"

"Absolutely."

I called the prep room and a door opened. The five men walked into the room, standing along its back wall.

"Take your time looking. We have all the time you need. When you want to see their profiles, just say the word."

I studied his face as he worked his way down the line. He paused at number three longer than the first two. *Shit.* He moved on quickly past number four to five. Was that a twitch? He stayed on him just as long as three, so we had a shot.

He worked his way back up the line and then said, "Can we ask them to turn, please?"

I hit the intercom. "Turn to your left, please."

The men rotated, showing their right-sided profile. I wanted the witness to give us a sign, but after a few seconds he said, "Can we get their other side? The side I saw when the guy was in the Explorer."

"Turn the other way, gentlemen."

As soon as the men displayed the left side of their profiles, the witness leaned into the window. He took more time going over the men but still breezed past the first two. He looked intently at number three again. I didn't get it. He looked nothing like Bellows.

He virtually skipped over the fourth man and peered at Bellows longer than he had at number three. The witness turned to Derrick. "Okay, I have seen enough."

## 49

—————

Derrick pulled me aside. "When you called me after leaving the ballpark to do background checks, I did."

"And what came up?"

"Smick was in Park Royal Behavioral less than a year ago."

"Park Royal? For what?"

"Bipolar disorder."

"We can't get the records while he was there."

"I know, but people with that disorder can be violent."

"How long was he there?"

"Sixty days."

"If he stopped taking his meds, he could have easily become violent."

"We should talk to this guy."

"No doubt, but I'm concerned if we spook him, he might ditch evidence."

"Do you want surveillance on him?"

"What I really want is to search his house and van. I saw something that looked weird in his van. Something like a dog, but it didn't move, like it was dead."

"That's more than weird."

"I'm going to call my buddy Tim Winters, and see if he can find out if Smick went into Park Royal under the Baker Act because he was a threat to somebody. And when he arrested Smick, if they swabbed him for DNA."

"What do you want me to do about Bellows?"

"You know, this eyewitness makes me nervous. If we need to make a case against him, we won't be able to use the lineup. He couldn't decide between Bellows and Bacchus. If we do, the defense will shred it into confetti."

"We don't have enough to get a search warrant, right?"

"All we have to give a judge is the angry husband angle. Why don't you trail him, see if you can lift some of his DNA?"

<hr>

"Hey, Frank, I checked into Eugene Smick for you."

"Thanks, Timmy. What do you have for me?"

"I know you know this, but you can't be broadcasting this, okay?"

"No problem."

"Smick was brought to Park Royal under the Baker Act. The officer made the determination and invoked the act. The officer was responding to a call a neighbor had made. Smick was apparently raging, threatening, and didn't make sense. He was going on that someone had dented his car and that it was one of the neighbors, and they knew who it was but wouldn't tell him. The officer tried to reason with him, but he kept repeating that he had a gun and was going to get his neighbors."

"Sad."

"When you brought him in for stalking Weaver, you took a DNA swab, right?"

"Yes, but here's the thing: since the law just went into effect this year, we've been taking the samples, but the lab is overloaded. They mandated taking it but never added the personnel to process it."

"Are you kidding me? We added two techs in Collier to handle it."

"We're averaging over sixty-five arrests a day."

"We're only about twenty a day."

"We'd need six techs, minimum, and they only added one."

"Anything you can do to bump it to the head of the line?"

"Without probable cause, there's nothing anybody can do. Unless you're the sheriff, of course. You know how that goes."

"I'm working on it. Thanks, Timmy, I really appreciate it."

SHOPPING FOR GROCERIES, I rolled around the chances a judge would agree to let me search the Bellows and Smick homes. It was just over zero. Asking for two at the same time proved the weakness in either man's culpability.

I checked the puttanesca recipe we made at the cooking class Mary Ann had given me for my birthday present. Slowly but surely my interest in cooking had escalated. I always loved eating out and appreciated the way restaurants prepared their versions of a dish, but before meeting Mary Ann, cooking was heating up soup or making grilled cheese.

I wasn't the creative type, but I could follow a recipe and liked turning raw ingredients into a meal. This dish was a spin on a traditional pasta dish named after the ladies of the night. It added tuna and cut back on the anchovies. I liked the way it went with Chianti.

Examining a bunch of vine-ripened tomatoes, my phone rang. It was Derrick.

"Can this wait? I'm in Publix."

"I snagged some DNA from Bellows."

"How'd you do that?"

"I followed him to the Panera by Old Forty-One. He had a sandwich and soda. I took the glass he used."

"He didn't see you, did he?"

"No. He was glued to his phone half the time."

"You get it to the lab?"

"On my way now."

"Good, I'll talk to you later."

"Hang on, there's more. They grabbed Jacques Redoux in Miami trying to board a flight to Marseille."

"Have they questioned him?"

"Not intently, they were waiting on us."

"Send me the contact details for the Homeland guys who are holding him."

Bagging two bunches of tomatoes, I rushed to the canned meat aisle. A couple of cans of tuna were going to have to do tonight, but I'd make it Progresso. Heading to the checkout I veered to the wine department. There was no time to stop at a wine store. I couldn't find a producer I recognized and grabbed a twenty-two-dollar bottle that had a nice black-and-gold label.

I barged into the house.

"I'm home."

"Daddy's home, Jessica. Let's give him a kiss hello."

I set the bag on the table, kissed Mary Ann and grabbed

my little girl. She had a pair of white overalls over a pink top. She was cute as hell. I gave her a kiss.

"You want to go for a horsey ride?"

Jessie smiled, and I put her on my shoulders, trotting through the house as Mary Ann unpacked the groceries. I came into the kitchen and Mary Ann said, "You didn't get any spaghetti."

"Shit!"

"Frank!" She took Jessica from me. "How many times do I have to tell you to watch your mouth?"

"I'm sorry. You don't know what's going on. My mind is fried with the Salter case. I'm juggling three suspects and the sh— everything is hitting the fan."

## 50

"WHY'D YOU OPEN THE BOTTLE IF YOU WEREN'T GOING TO drink it?"

I didn't want to tell her that I was waiting for a chance to leave the house and get back to finding Salter's killer.

"I guess I'm just preoccupied with the case."

"It's like you're not even here. Jessica's trying to show you she's eating, and you're not paying attention to her."

"Sorry, there's so much to do—"

"We agreed not to bring it home. Remember, family time is family time."

"I know, but—"

"You'll get it done, Frank. Drink the wine and relax. Tomorrow will be here before you know it."

I poured a glassful and took a big gulp before chopping a string of spaghetti up for Jessie.

It was a good thing I caught a buzz from drinking the entire bottle; it was the only thing that kept me from sneaking out of the house.

The next morning I was at my desk before eight, drafting a request to search both Bellows' and Smick's houses. We had to be ready to act as soon as we had more than strong suspicions. I printed both and laid them on Derrick's desk with a note that I'd call with instructions.

I had tried to find a way to link Bellows and Smick but gave up trying to get a judge to let me search both apartments.

Traveling on Daniels Parkway there were plenty of signs for JetBlue Stadium. Smick lived near the stadium. When I made my way down Epping Way, I realized just how close he was. The stadium's parking lot began a couple of yards from the end of his street. In back of his apartment complex was an office building that headquartered Crystex Electronics.

I pulled into the lot and immediately saw Smick's van. It was 9:30 a.m., and there was only one spot open. Didn't anyone work? The door to a small lobby was locked. A woman holding a baby came out of a door and headed toward the back of the building. I took my phone out and sent a text to Derrick, telling him where I was.

When I looked up, Smick was in the hallway closing his door. He stuck a series of keys into the door; there seemed to be three locks. I took a step back as Smick looked at me. He headed in the direction the woman had.

I jogged back to the parking lot. Smick, in a red baseball cap, was twenty feet from his van.

"Mr. Smick? Eugene Smick?"

He turned around. "Yeah. What do you want?"

I pulled my badge out. "Detective Luca, sheriff's department."

He rubbed a hand over the stubble on his cheek but said nothing. His eyes were glassy.

"I wanted to ask you a couple of questions."

Smick wore work boots and grease-smeared chinos. "Oh, come on, I need my coffee, man."

"Late night?"

"I need my coffee before I go to work."

One of his legs was shaking rapidly. "I'll be quick."

He sighed heavily. "Oh, man. I need my damn coffee. You don't understand."

"You like living by the stadium?"

He smiled. "Oh yeah, it's good, but I hate it when spring training's over. Only four days left now. Man, I wish there was like a thousand more days. Did you know one of the practice fields, the one to the left of the stadium, it has the same dimensions as Fenway Park. How cool is that?"

"I didn't know that."

"Are we done?"

"A couple of days ago I was at the game, the one against the Yankees."

"We won that game. Nice comeback. Brecker hit a double, and then Martinez brought him home to tie it. There were two out when they tied it. I was getting really nervous—"

"You got into it with Ron Weaver over the team losing Blair."

He stood on his toes. "That was a complete fuck up! They're goddamn morons. Blair is the best center fielder. They want to give me the bullshit Sanchez coming up is going to fill his shoes? Total bullshit. That's what it is. Blair, he hit two eighty-nine, had twenty-seven doubles, fourteen homers, his on-base percentage is three eighty-three."

I pointed to his vehicle. "I saw the bumper stickers on your van about moving the team out of Fort Myers."

"It was one of the stupidest things the team would have done. We won't let it happen."

"What do you mean by, we won't let it happen?"

"The fans. It's our team. Without us they got nothing."

"I understand the new stadium would have had a bunch of amenities and would be larger than the one here."

"Who needs amenities? The corporations? They'll ruin it for us. This place is not even ten years old. We have six extra fields here. Plus rehab facilities for when a player gets injured. Last year, when Jimenez hurt his shoulder, he was here almost all of June. I got to talk to him a bunch of times. We became good friends. And the GLC Red Sox play here all summer long."

"Do you know Elby Salter?"

Smick blinked. "No."

"He was the businessman behind the effort to move the team. Salter owned the property the new stadium was going to be built on."

"I never heard of him. I got to go. I'm late."

Smick climbed into his van and drove off. I walked around the building trying to identify which windows belonged to his apartment.

<h1 style="text-align:center">51</h1>

WE HAD BEEN REQUIRED TO TAKE COURSES CONCERNING THE possibility that someone we encountered was suffering from mental illness. The curriculum only provided an overview, but it was eye-opening.

I could visualize the instructor but couldn't come up with her name. I grabbed the binder we'd used in the class out of the bottom of my credenza. Right on the cover was her name and contact information: Norma Wiedner, a certified member of the American Board of Psychiatry and Neurology.

"Dr. Wiedner, this is Detective Luca with the Collier County Sheriff's Office. We met at the public safety conference in Orlando. I took your class and learned quite a bit from it."

"Thank you. What division are you with?"

"Homicide."

"I see. How can I help you?"

"We have a case, and frankly I'm not sure this line of inquiry is even related, but learning more about your field can't hurt."

"It certainly couldn't. I wish more law enforcement agencies had vigorous programs to educate their staff on mental illness. What would you like to know?"

"I'm trying to understand something about bipolar disorder. We have someone who was admitted to a facility for treatment of bipolar disorder."

"How would you know that? That information is confidential."

"There was a domestic disturbance, and the individual was threatening to harm his neighbors, forcing the officer to invoke the Baker Act."

"That worked as the law intended it to, but any diagnosis made by the receiving facility is private. How did you obtain the patient's records?"

"The individual made a voluntary disclosure when he was arrested on an unrelated offense."

"I see."

"There is a chance he could have murdered someone, but the motivation doesn't appear to be a strong one. What can you tell me about this illness?"

"A diagnosis of bipolar does not mean that someone is violent. In fact, more violence is committed against people with mental illnesses than by those suffering from it. Untreated, it is a degenerative disorder and can lead to psychosis."

"A loss of contact with reality?"

"Yes. The risks are higher if substance abuse is involved or if the person is unemployed."

Smick had a job. Was he on drugs? "Makes sense."

"Based on what you said, it unfortunately appears that this individual had at least one manic episode. Left untreated, there is a high rate of recurrence."

"Can you go over what a manic episode is?"

"A state of heightened overall activation with enhanced expression."

"Sorry, Doc, can you put that into English?"

"Elevated moods. They can be euphoric or irritable. As the mania intensifies, the irritability can be more pronounced, leading to the possibility of violence. Many sufferers also experience blackouts. They have no memory or recall ability when they have an episode."

"If someone was treated, say for a sixty-day period, but had stopped taking their medicines, would that bring it on?"

"I'm afraid so. Medication adherence is a serious problem overall but especially acute when dealing with mental illness. The estimate is nearly sixty percent of patients are nonadherent. It's a shame, taking the prescribed drugs would help to control their disorder."

"Just curious, would longer stays in a facility increase the rate that people would take their medicines?"

"Yes, but all that anybody seems to care about is that the cost of care in a certified environment is more than four times the cost of imprisonment."

"I didn't know that."

"It's true but completely misleading. If someone commits a crime that was preventable by treating their mental illness, they'll go to prison for years and years. We need to measure the cost of treatment against the costs of a ten-year imprisonment."

She was dead-on. Short-term financial pain for long-term gain, and not just in the monetary sense. I wanted to continue the discussion, but I had a killer to track down.

ALLIGATOR ALLEY WAS EMPTY. I slowed down from doing eighty-five as I approached the section that ran through the Miccosukee Indian Reservation. I didn't want to get into anything with one of their patrol cars. While checking the speedometer an idea hit me, and I called my partner.

"Derrick, put the warrant request in on Smick."

"You sure?"

"Look, Smick's DNA is in a backlog up in Lee. We're going to get Bellows' DNA results from our lab faster. That way we're moving on both fronts."

"Shouldn't I put something in the request about the backup in Lee County? The judge might be sympathetic."

"No way. It's not about sympathy; it's about probable cause. If a judge knows we're waiting on a DNA sample, he's going to make us sit on our hands until it comes in."

"Good point. How close are you to Miami?"

"More than halfway."

## 52

I watched the video feed of Jacques Redoux as he was escorted out of Miami Airport's sizable detention area. He seemed to be joking with the Homeland Security guards and had a smile on his face. He had shaven off his beard. I made my way to an interview room with two bottles of water.

The drab space was by an area where a handful of customs inspectors were going through luggage. The smell of sweat hung in the air. Questions and answers were being exchanged in several different languages.

The Frenchman came in with his blue sports jacket slung over his shoulder. His white shirt was heavily wrinkled as were his gray slacks. Deeply tanned, Redoux had an easy manner to him, a hotel-concierge style.

I introduced myself and asked the guards to wait outside. We took seats across a metal desk. He had less of an accent than his cousin Marie.

"I do hope we can put an end to this misunderstanding."

I didn't drive two hours and change, over a misunderstanding. "What was the purpose of your visit to the United States?"

"It was time for some fun and sun."

"Where did you stay?"

"At the Marseilles Hotel."

There was a hotel in Miami with the same name as the French town his crime ring was connected with? I needed to process that.

"Let me see the receipt."

As he was opening his wallet, he said, "Oh, that was last time. I forgot all about it. It must be the lack of sleep. As you can imagine, I failed to sleep last night."

The bill was from the Pestana South Beach. I had stayed there a few years ago. It was right by the Miami Beach Convention Center. Driving here, I passed several billboards advertising the Basel Art Show. It was one of the biggest contemporary art shows in the country.

"Did you go to the art show?"

"Art? No, that's not for me."

"Your uncle, Lucien, seems to have a strong interest in it."

"I wouldn't know."

"Why don't we stop pretending you were here on vacation."

"I'm sorry that I don't understand what the American authorities think I have done."

"Did you visit your cousin Marie?"

"She is in New York, no?"

"Do you know Elby Salter?"

He shook his head. "No. I don't know him."

I handed him a photo of Salter. He took it and gave it a good look. "Is this the Salter man?"

"Yes."

He handed it back. "I never saw this man."

I cracked open a bottle of water. "Would you like one?"

"Yes. Thank you."

We took swigs, and I had my DNA, not that it would do me much good if he were in France. The forty-eight-hour detention period was coming to a close, and he knew it.

"Family honor is a big thing in France, isn't it?"

"Of course. But we are not the only people who value family."

"When someone attacks or hurts a member of the family, you take that seriously, right?"

"Of course. These are basic questions. I am sorry, Mr. Detective, but I don't understand the American technique. Why have I been detained?"

"Did your cousin Marie ask you, your uncle, or anyone else in your family to avenge a wrong against Marie's daughter?"

"Marie's daughter? What happened?"

"We believe she may have been sexually assaulted."

His shoulders collapsed. "By who? Who is the bastard?"

I pointed to the picture of Salter.

He was hiding something, but his body language told me it had nothing to do with Salter. It wasn't a waste of time; I had to see this guy for myself. I asked several more questions before turning him back over to Homeland Security.

I didn't lift our hold on him. He was up to something, and I would use the long drive ahead to try and figure it out.

# 53

Derrick confirmed Smick was working. It was perfect. We wouldn't have to contend with any bitching while we searched. We pulled into the parking lot behind two marked cars. Before we got our gear out, three residents had stepped out of the building to see what was going on.

As a precaution, I knocked on Smick's door as Derrick went to get a key from the manager. Two officers stood on both ends of the hallway to keep the residents away.

Derrick unlocked the door, but there were two other locks the manager had no keys for. He sorted through the department's collection of bump keys and pulled out two that matched the locks. Within five minutes, he swung the door open.

I was hit with an unmistakable odor—the smell of a man living alone. Before entering, I flicked on the lights, scanning the visible areas.

Dominated by what looked like a seventy-inch TV, the main room looked in the midst of being repainted. A wall and a half had blue paint covering what had been tan. A framed poster of Carlton Fisk persuading a ball to stay fair leaned against a wall.

We walked in toward a ladder in a corner of the room. On its top step was a roller crusted with dried paint. It'd been months since it'd been dipped in a pan that had hardened paint in it.

Derrick said, "What's that all about? Finish the wall before you're going to abandon it."

"I think it's related to his condition. I read that people with bipolar disorder have bursts of energy where they tackle projects but never complete them as their mood changes."

A Red Sox throw was on the back of a worn corduroy couch. Baseball scorecards were stacked on the corner of the coffee table.

"Start in here, Derrick."

I walked in the kitchen. The fridge was covered with an assortment of Red Sox magnets. A partially completed jigsaw puzzle on the table was covered with mail, a dirty bowl, and a spoon. I pulled open a few drawers and went to the master bedroom.

No headboard, and the bed was unmade. I went straight to the nightstand, yanking open its drawer. No handgun but plenty of empty pill bottles. I pulled on gloves and picked up one. It was something called Lamictal. The prescription was over a year old.

There were three other bottles each of Seroquel and Abilify. All were empty. Unless he was carrying around his pills, Smick was off his meds. I took a photo and closed the drawer.

A monitor and keyboard sat on a metal desk covered with papers. They were tax forms for the year 2015. I slid open the only drawer. Lying on top of a *Sports Illustrated* magazine was a handgun. A .357 revolver. I lifted it with my pen and bagged it. There was nothing else of interest, unless you were into collecting baseball cards or autographs.

I opened the closet. It looked lonely. Two pairs of jeans and chinos were hanging next to a button-down shirt. The shelf, however, was crammed with goods. We'd have to give that a thorough look.

Derrick was looking in a kitchen cabinet when I came in holding the bagged gun.

"It's a .357 revolver."

"You think it's the murder weapon?"

"I don't know what to think, except to get it tested immediately."

I called the lab and handed the gun off to an officer to run it to them for testing.

---

We were passing the Hertz Arena when Derrick received a call. It was about a body.

"Looks like we might have an ID on the Naples Dock body."

"Who is it?"

"They think it's a Bahamian that was reported missing. Guy called Abreu."

"From the Bahamas?"

"Yep, he matches the description, including the tattoo. It was in Portuguese."

"How the hell did he end up shot in the back of the head?"

"Looks like Abreu was into drug running, and who knows what he did."

"If it's drug related and international, Chester will hand it off."

"I thought for sure it had some connection to Redoux."

"Call the lab; see where they are with ballistics."

He called. "Not yet."

"What the hell is taking so long?"

"They said it'd be finished in no more than two hours."

My pee alarm went off. I was doing my best not to ignore it any longer. Besides, we had a couple of hours to kill.

"I have to take a leak. A buddy of mine works at Mattress City off Immokalee. The bathrooms are clean there."

Derrick waited in the car. My friend was talking a couple into a three-thousand-dollar mattress. I waved and headed to the boy's room.

It was as clean as I remembered it. Why did a mattress company put so much effort into keeping their toilets pristine while many grocery stores didn't?

Sitting on the throne, I tickled my abdomen to try to get a trickle going. I tried to weigh the odds that we had the gun that killed Salter. Why would someone keep a murder weapon in a desk drawer?

Smick had mental issues and had been hospitalized for threatening his neighbors. On the other hand, he held a job that demonstrated he could be responsible. Why wouldn't he ditch it or at least hide it if it was the gun that killed Salter?

Doubt started to build as my flow increased. Smick had a van that required registration and insurance. We needed to get a look inside his vehicle. I thought of Elby Salter's car and the fact that the junkyard controlled by Hamlet had never produced the correct documentation. What was Hamlet hiding?

Come on, Luca. Think. What is it? Pull it out, Luca. Then

I remembered something that my own name triggered: Lucayan Holdings, a business name that came up when I did a company search related to Hamlet.

Could there be a connection? They were located in the Bahamas. You know how I feel about coincidences.

## 54

Trying to be discreet wasn't working, so I waved my badge in her face, and Hamlet's screener collapsed like a cheap beach umbrella. Since Derrick was going to let me know when the ballistics report came in, I kept my phone on vibrate.

The woman went to tell Hamlet and disappeared faster than free food samples at Publix. The "1812 Overture" playing in the background almost made me laugh out loud.

A minute had barely passed before Hamlet lumbered down the hallway. His Rudolph nose was visible from thirty feet away. He pointed to a room and entered. Heads lifted from workstations as I followed him. Hamlet was standing in the same conference room we'd met in before.

"Detective, I'm doing the best I can to locate the documentation on Elby's vehicle."

"Good, but I'm here on another matter."

He tugged the cuff of his sleeve. "Please, have a seat. What's this about?"

"Your Bahamian business interests."

He wet his lips. "What about them?"

A text came in. It was from Derrick. There was no ballistic match. The gun in Smick's apartment wasn't the murder weapon. Damn it.

"I'd like to know what they do."

"Well, Caribbean Solutions is our largest business. Mainly they are focused on upgrading and installing technology solutions for the private and public sectors. CS, as we call it, has several contracts with the Bahamian government."

"Do they work with the banks down there?"

"You couldn't avoid it if you want to survive. Financial services is right behind tourism in the islands."

"And Bahamian Enterprises?"

"They're focused on the basic needs of the people. Nothing exotic. We have the third largest grocery chain, though it's something we're looking at exiting. It's just too competitive, and the margins are paper thin."

"And what about Lucayan Holdings?" Pronouncing it Luc-uh-yan.

"Luc-a-yan Holdings is tourism centered. We have interests in a couple of smaller hotels as well as several excursion and water sport entities throughout the Bahamian chain."

My phone vibrated. It was the retired reporter again. She had called two times before. I swiped the call away. "You rent out boats, don't you?"

"Yes, along with parasailing, fishing trips, jet skis, and taking people on tours. We also operate an interisland transport service. Those types of things."

"You had some legal issues with it, didn't you?"

"Uhm. I'm not sure what you're referring to."

"Wasn't Lucayan sanctioned by the Bahamian authorities for its involvement in a drug smuggling ring?"

"Oh, that. It was a renegade employee who used one of our boats without permission. Frankly, we should have pressed charges against him for theft. We were unfortunately caught up in it."

"There seems to be a pattern, as it was the second time, as you say, that you were caught up in a smuggling crime."

"We were exonerated of any responsibility in both instances."

"But you paid significant fines. I'd say that sounds like you were complicit."

"It was easier to pay a fine than fight it. Things don't work the same in the Bahamas. So, we decided to get it behind us. We also tightened our hiring practices significantly, even though finding quality employees is a struggle throughout the Caribbean."

"Thanks to a couple of favors from friends who work for the feds, I've seen the settlement documentation. It's not quite as you say it is." I hadn't seen it, but Hamlet had no idea of what kind of access we might have, and I needed a breakthrough.

"We admitted to minor offenses."

"You have partners in your Bahamian businesses, right?"

"We partner all the time, especially in places like the Caribbean, where locals can be the difference between success and failure."

"You do that frequently with the Salter family, don't you?"

"Yes, among others."

"The others in your monthly meeting group?"

"Going into business and doing deals with entities that have similar goals and attributes isn't a violation of law."

I decided to take a shot. "I understand some of your poker buddies are involved in the Bahamas as well."

"We have minority partners in many of our investments."

"Are the Salters partners in any of your Bahamian companies?"

"You couldn't expect me to keep track of details like that. We have almost three hundred investment vehicles and scores of partners."

He knew damn well whether or not Salter was involved. Hamlet was hiding Elby Salter's involvement. The questions began to bubble. Was there a connection between the secret group and drug smuggling? Did an outsider make an example out of Salter? Or did Elby Salter find out about the covert activities, made a stink about it, and was killed to silence him?

We had never explored the narcotics angle. The way Salter was killed dovetailed with the way drug players did business. The DEA might have something on one of the companies the Salters owned.

Leaving Hamlet's office, my mind was spinning. Hamlet was sending cars to China. Did he or any other group members have shipments coming into the country, shipments that could be used to cover imported drugs?

By the time I jumped into the Cherokee, my enthusiasm waned. A large drug ring was a stretch. These people were wealthy already. Why would they risk it? But there was the drug smuggling charge. Not one, but two of them.

Waiting for a chance to pull onto Route 41, a car swung into the lot. The driver looked familiar. It was Tony Bellows. I shifted into reverse. There was a car in back of me. I waved, but the driver did nothing.

I opened the door and jumped out. Badge in the air, I said, "Move out of the way! Now!"

Tires screeching, I backed up. Putting the car into drive, I watched Bellows enter the building. He disappeared into an elevator. By the time I got to the lobby, the elevator was on the way back down.

I studied the directory of companies in the four-story building. Hamlet Holdings took up one floor. The balance of firms were financial advisers, law firms, and accountants.

Bellows and Hamlet. What was the connection? Could the ex-cop be the hired hit man? Were these prominent men that smart? They'd found out about Bellows' wife and used him to take care of whatever problem they had with Salter?

Where the hell were the DNA results on Bellows? I pulled out my cell, ready to rip the guys in the lab a couple of new assholes, when the phone vibrated in my hand. It was the lab.

## 55

---

WE HAD A DNA MATCH. IT WAS TIME TO BRING HIM IN. I always made sure the team knew how I wanted an arrest to be carried out. It was going to be Derrick and me along with four officers. It might have been overkill, but showing up with an overwhelming force was usually effective insurance. We were gathered in my office. I handed each member a sketch of the location.

"I don't want anybody taking any chances. This guy has demonstrated he'll kill. If he feels cornered, there's no telling what he might do."

Derrick said, "Frank and I will take the front."

"And I want two covering the rear and one on each side. I don't care how hot it is, everyone in body armor."

A minor groan was covered by the ring of my cell phone. It was Mary Ann. I hit an automatic text response and said, "I don't believe anyone will be with him, but we can never be certain." My phone rang again. It was Mary Ann again. "Sorry, let me get this."

"Mary Ann, I'm in the middle—"

"We're at the hospital. Jessica fell—"

"Is she all right?"

"Hit the back of her head. It was a hard fall. She's bleeding but not badly."

"Where are you?"

"NCH on Immokalee."

"I'll get there as soon as I can."

"You don't have to come, Frank. I just wanted you to know. She'll be fine."

"You sure?"

"Yes. I'll call you later."

I hung up. Derrick said, "What's the matter?"

"Jessie fell and hit her head. They're in the emergency room. I gotta go."

"Don't worry, Frank. We have this handled. I'll get Reilly to come along. Go take care of your family."

He did have it under control. "I owe you, man, thanks. And be careful."

---

"HOW'S JESSICA?"

"She's amazing. Didn't need stitches, just a butterfly thing. She didn't even cry when they shaved the back of her head. Me and Mary Ann were leaking tears, but she was playing with the doctor's stethoscope."

"Good scare, huh?"

"You got that right. They're a little concerned about a concussion, so we'll keep an eye on her tonight, just to be safe."

"I'm sure she'll be fine."

"You ready to get this done?"

"Can't wait."

I rapped on the door and swung it open. It was the first

time since I'd learned the tactics of interviewing that I hadn't made the room uncomfortable for a suspect.

Eugene Smick was chewing on a cuticle.

"Mr. Smick, I'm Detective Frank Luca, and this is Detective Derrick Dickson."

"I remember you. You were at my house."

"That's right. Would you mind answering a couple of questions for us?"

He shrugged. "Can't you take these off?"

"It's protocol, but I'll tell you what I'll do. I can remove one of them. Which one you want off?"

He raised his right arm. "This one."

Derrick recited the formalities. I unhooked a cuff and said, "You have the right to have a lawyer present during this interview."

"I don't need one."

"Do you know why you were arrested?"

"I didn't do anything."

"Your DNA was found on Elby Salter's body and in his vehicle. Can you explain how that came to be?"

"Anything is possible today with technology."

"You knew it was Mr. Salter who was behind the effort to move the team out of Fort Myers."

"It was a stupid fucking idea."

"And you didn't want that to happen, did you? You live so close to JetBlue Stadium."

"I told them not to do it. I sent letters, but nobody was listening to me. And it wasn't just me. You know there were millions of fans who didn't want them to move. Not even one was okay with it."

I noticed a tremor in his left hand. "Why did you stop taking your medicines?"

"They didn't do nothing. And they cost a lot of money for nothing."

"The county is going to pay for a supply while you're in custody."

"How long am I gonna be in here?"

"Your lawyer can tell you that."

"What time is it?"

"Two fifteen."

He jumped to his feet. "I'm missing the game. You got to get me out of here. I didn't do anything. I can't miss one. I never missed a game in my life."

"We can't do that just yet, but let me see what I can do about seeing it on TV."

---

WE STEPPED into the hall and Derrick said, "That's it, Frank?"

"We did our job, kiddo. This is way above us. We have enough physical evidence, including the murder weapon you found in his van. Pushing someone like him to confess is just going to agitate him. He's going to be evaluated, and at this point he'll be institutionalized for the criminally insane."

"And we thought it was Fred Baylor working for Hamlet."

"I know. I never would have guessed he was just getting his taxes done."

"You think if Smick were taking his meds, he wouldn't have killed Salter?"

"I don't know, but the doctors seem to think so."

"Maybe one day with technology they'll find a way to implant a device like they do with some diabetes patients."

"That's a damn good point. Why haven't they developed something like that?"

My cell rang. It was the old reporter, Rosanne Roberts. "Let me get this."

"Ms. Roberts, how are you? I'm sorry I didn't get back to you, but it's been hectic."

"That's okay. At my age, you learn to wait."

"What can I do for you?"

"I did some more digging. After I told you about those two incidents, I just had to see what I could find. Well, anyhow, there was this woman, Matthews, who filed a—"

"Yes, we know about her, but she wouldn't talk because of an NDA."

"Oh, okay, but did you know that this woman did the same thing to two other men?"

"She accused them of sexual impropriety with her daughter?"

"Yep, looks like she was able to get both of them to pay her to keep silent. I don't know for sure, but this thing with Elby Salter looks groundless."

The comfort that a case of pedophilia hadn't happened was eroded by knowing that someone had made baseless charges of the highest order and had gotten away with it.

## 56

Annabelle was talking with a woman who had a group of children lined up behind her. She pointed to an exhibit. The woman nodded and led her kids away.

Annabelle smiled when she noticed me and scooted over, saying, "It's busy this morning."

"How are you doing?"

"I'm actually doing quite well. The move went as smoothly as moves do, and I like my new place."

"That's good. I know how difficult it can be to go forward."

"I'm not going to kid you; it's an adjustment, but you find out who your real friends are."

"I bet you did."

"Funny thing is, I'm actually happier than I've been in a long while."

"Good for you. I wanted to come by personally and share something that I learned about Elby."

She took a tiny step back. "Oh. What is that?"

"As you know, there was a sexual complaint filed against

him and whispers of impropriety that we uncovered during the investigation."

Her frown lengthened.

"Well, it turns out that the woman who filed the complaint has a history of doing that sort of thing. She filed the same charge against two other men. I don't know if that's any comfort to you, but I did want you to know it appears baseless."

"You don't know how much I appreciate that. As you can imagine, the entire episode was disturbing. I wanted to believe Elby, but in the back of my mind I had doubts."

"That's completely normal. I'm sorry for anything we may have inferred during the investigation, but it was something that we had to pursue."

"Elby had his faults, but something like that would have been unforgivable."

It was nice to bring good news to Annabelle. She had been through some difficult times, but it looked like she was going to be fine.

I also thought Chadwick deserved to know that his brother wasn't a pedophile. Pulling out my phone, I dialed his number.

## 57

SEEKING PROSECUTORIAL LENIENCY, SMICK'S PUBLIC defender helped us obtain a full confession. But knowing the details didn't give me the satisfaction I usually experienced getting the particulars of a crime.

Instead, I felt down and left the office. It wouldn't make a difference, would it? No matter what I did, I couldn't keep people like Smick from doing what he did.

I SURPRISED Mary Ann by coming home early. Jessie was sleeping in her playpen.

"You got the Smick confession?"

"Yep, all the depressing details."

"What happened?"

"He pulled a gun on Salter in the stadium's parking lot and got in his SUV. He said they drove around for hours."

"Poor guy must have been scared out of his mind."

"Salter tried to pay Smick off, went to an ATM and gave him three thousand to let him go. But it didn't work. Smick made Salter get in the back seat and tied him up. Then he shot

Salter at a red light on Livingston and Vanderbilt. Can you believe it? Sitting at a damn red light."

"God. How terrible."

"Sick, that's what it is. After dumping Salter, he drove to where he works, cleaned up and screwed with the motor to make it look like it was seizing up. Smick poured muriatic acid on the vehicle and sold it to Carmine's Scrap Yard."

"So sad."

"I don't know; this one really got to me."

"Well, it's over now."

I shrugged. "Maybe I'm getting too old for this job. It might be time to move upstairs."

"You? Behind a desk?"

"Why not?"

"What's going on, Frank?"

"I don't know. I want the world that Jessie grows up in to be safe, to be a better place than the one I grew up in."

"And you're helping to do that."

"That's nonsense. What do I do? Clean up after the shit hits the fan. That's what I do. I can't prevent things like this happening. No matter what I do, people are going to do crazy things."

"You're not God, Frank. You do what you can. Don't kid yourself. What you do makes a difference. Without you, many of these murderers would be still out there."

"Maybe. I'm going to get changed."

I hopped in the shower, hoping to wash the grime of the case off me.

---

MARY ANN WAS PUTTING Jessica's feet in the pool while I finished prepping for dinner. A recipe for a fig sauce I had read about for ribs sounded too good not to try on a day like today. I basted the ribs, covered them with foil and went to get a bottle of wine. The chef recommended a big wine, so I took out a California Syrah.

Uncorking the bottle, the house phone rang. No one ever called us on it. I patted my pants; where was my phone? Thinking someone may have tried my cell, I answered it.

It was a woman. "Detective Luca?"

"Yes. Who is this?"

"Hold on a second. Mr. Salter would like to speak to you."

Chadwick was calling me?

"Mr. Luca, this is Prescott Salter calling. I wanted to thank you for bringing our family a measure of closure with the arrest of his killer."

"I appreciate that, but I'm just doing my job, sir."

"Well, we're grateful. If we can do anything for you or the department, please don't hesitate to ask."

"Thank you. There is something I'd like you to consider, since you are active in the charitable arena."

"We believe it's our obligation to help others."

"I ask this not just because of the circumstances of your son's murder, but in a general sense. And I'm not saying other causes are not worthy, but mental health does not attract the same number of dollars that, say, cancer research does. The entire field could use some help, be it awareness, treatment, research, access, you name it; there is a need."

"That's an interesting, unselfish request, Detective. Your mother did a fine job raising you."

"I lost her too early, sir, but that's another story. Thank you for your call."

.  .  .

TWO DAYS LATER, I was watching the news while grilling portobello mushrooms. I smiled when the newscaster reported that an anonymous donor had donated $10 million to the Mental Health Association of Southwest Florida.

---

The next book in this series is, A Killer Missteps. Find it in eBook, Paperback, and Audio.

I hope you enjoyed reading this book as much as I enjoyed writing it. If you did, I'd appreciate it if you would write a quick review on Amazon or your favorite book site. Reviews are an author's best friend and even a quick line or two is helpful. Thanks, Dan

# OTHER BOOKS BY DAN

Complicit Witness

Push Back

Ambition Cliff


You can keep abreast of my writing and have access to books that are free of discounting by joining my newsletter. It normally is out once a month and also contains notes on self- esteem, motivational pieces and wine articles.

It's free. See bottom of my website: www.danpetrosini.com

# ABOUT THE AUTHOR

Dan is a USA Today and Amazon best-selling author who wrote his first story at the age of ten and enjoys telling a story or joke.

Dan gets his story ideas by exploring the question; What if?

In almost every situation he finds himself in, Dan explores what if this or that happened? What if this person died or did something unusual or illegal?

Dan's non-stop mind spin provides him with plenty of material to weave into interesting stories.

A fan of books and films that have twists and are difficult to predict, Dan crafts his stories to prevent readers from guessing correctly. He writes every day, forcing the words out when necessary and has written over twenty-five novels to date.

It's not a matter of wanting to write, Dan simply has to.

Dan passionately believes people can realize their dreams if they focus and act, and he encourages just that.

His favorite saying is – "The price of discipline is always less than the cost of regret"

Dan reminds people to get the negativity out of their lives. He believes it is contagious and advises people to steer clear of negative people. He knows having a true, positive mind set makes it feel like life is rigged in your favor. When he gets off base, he tells himself, 'You can't have a good day with a bad attitude.'

Married with two daughters and a needy Maltese, Dan lives in Southwest Florida. A New York native, Dan has taught at local colleges, writes novels, and plays tenor saxophone in several jazz bands. He also drinks way too much wine and never, ever takes himself too seriously.

He puts out a twice-a-month newsletter featuring articles, his writing and special deals and steals.

Sign up at www.danpetrosini.com

www.ingramcontent.com/pod-product-compliance
Lightning Source LLC
Chambersburg PA
CBHW071211210726
48293CB00002B/376